Emily Tennyson (Bradley) Smith

Life of the Lady Arabella Stuart

Vol. I

Emily Tennyson (Bradley) Smith

Life of the Lady Arabella Stuart
Vol. I

ISBN/EAN: 9783744750295

Printed in Europe, USA, Canada, Australia, Japan

Cover: Foto ©Raphael Reischuk / pixelio.de

More available books at **www.hansebooks.com**

LIFE OF

THE LADY

ARABELLA STUART.

IN TWO PARTS: CONTAINING A BIOGRAPHICAL MEMOIR,
AND A COLLECTION OF HER LETTERS, WITH NOTES AND
DOCUMENTS FROM ORIGINAL SOURCES, RELATING.
TO HER HISTORY.

E. T. BRADLEY. Smith

IN TWO VOLUMES.
VOL. I.

LONDON:

RICHARD BENTLEY AND SON,

Publishers in Ordinary to Her Majesty the Queen.

1889.

DEDICATED

TO

MY FATHER,

THE DEAN OF WESTMINSTER,

AND TO

MY UNCLE,

SIR GEORGE GROVE.

PREFACE.

THE plea of a new and untrodden path of history cannot be urged as the excuse of the present memoir. Other feet have trodden the same way before, but nevertheless there are many bye-lanes and turnings which have hitherto been overlooked or undiscovered. Much still remains obscure, hidden, no doubt, in private collections; but the object of this biography is attained if the Lady Arabella, as she lived and suffered, is placed clearly before the reader.

Miss Costello, in " Eminent Englishwomen," and Disraeli in " Curiosities of Literature," led the way in noticing this romantic episode of history. Miss Cooper was, however, the first to attempt a biography and collection of letters. To her I owe much in the present volumes, notably the guidance to various authorities and references, and, through Canon Jackson, to the discovery made by her at the Bodleian of William Seymour's "Confession," which I have since seen and copied myself from the original.

To Canon Jackson I owe much, he having generously allowed me to see and use the fruits of many years' labour at Longleat. Through his researches Hugh Crompton, Arabella's steward, takes his proper place in her life and fate. In his copy of the "History of Great Bedwyn," I found the names of Crompton and also of Edward Kirton as Members of Parliament for Great Bedwyn (the former in 1623-4 and the latter in 1627), and the notice of their burials in the church there, where also is the family vault of William Seymour, whose daughter Arabella lies beside him. Hugh Crompton died in August, 1645, and Kirton in 1654, before the man in whose early troubles they had taken part.

To Mr. Inderwick's courtesy I owe the use of one or two details (duly acknowledged in the text) from his "Side-Lights on the Stuarts," which was published shortly before my book was in the press.

The new materials from the Cecil papers, never before seen by any biographer of Arabella, I have been allowed to use by the kindness of the Marquess of Salisbury.

Throughout the book, with very few exceptions, the old spelling has been altered to the modern standard, as the variable spelling of the time lends an illiterate appearance to letters written by the most highly educated people.

For the illustrations I am indebted to the kindness of friends ; to Mrs. Hogge, for the loan of her precious miniature ; to Mr. Cecil G. S. Foljambe, M.P., for his drawings of the Lenox coat-of-arms on the cover of the book, and of the seals used by Arabella.

I wish also to acknowledge a debt of gratitude —which cannot unfortunately now be personally expressed—to the late Mr. Selby of the Record Office, to whom I owe my first initiation into the deciphering of manuscripts.

For the invariable kindness and courtesy received on all sides during researches at the British and Kensington Museums, at the Record Office, and also at the London Library, as well as from friends, I beg to offer here my best thanks.

E. T. BRADLEY.

DEANERY, WESTMINSTER,
October, 1889.

CONTENTS OF VOL. I.

CHAPTER III.

EDUCATION, AND FIRST APPEARANCE AT COURT.

1582-1590.

CHAPTER IV.

JESUIT PLOTS AND MARRIAGE PROJECTS.

1590-1602.

CHAPTER VII.

THE LAST DAYS OF ELIZABETH.

1603.

CHAPTER VIII.

THE NEW COURT.

1603.

CHAPTER IX.

ARABELLA AS A COURT FAVOURITE.

1604-1607.

CHAPTER X.

THE FIRST CLOUD.

1608-1610.

CHAPTER XI.

A STOLEN MARRIAGE.

1610.

LIST OF ILLUSTRATIONS.

PART I.
MEMOIR.

—◆◆◆—

CHAPTER I.

INTRODUCTORY.

ERRATA.

Vol. I., p. 190, line 7 from bottom, also Vol. II., p. 188, line 17, *for* "nature's" *read* "native."

Vol. II., p. 283, line 4 from bottom, *for* "brother" *read* "son," and *for* "uncle" *read* "brother."

they were, of a love-marriage were granted perforce, since the crime of her wedding to the

•

CHAPTER XI.

A STOLEN MARRIAGE.

1610.

PART I.

MEMOIR.

—•◦•—

CHAPTER I.

INTRODUCTORY.

In former days, and even in modern times, the course of true love has not always run smoothly, especially for those who have royal blood in their veins.

To any one who has studied the history of Elizabeth and James I., two striking examples, both connected with the royal family, must at once occur.

The story of Katharine Grey is one of the most pathetic in history, only equalled by that of the subject of this memoir, Arabella Stuart.

To the one, however, the joys, brief though they were, of a love-marriage were granted perforce, since the crime of her wedding to the

young Earl of Hertford was not discovered till
many months had passed, and even after the
unfortunate pair were imprisoned in the Tower
they were allowed, by the kindness and com-
passion of their gaolers, to meet in secret. But
for the other lady, after a youth overshadowed
by the penalties consequent on her nearness to
the throne, love and happiness dawned only
to be crushed as their promises were about to
be fulfilled, and, hopelessly divided from her
husband, after a marriage they had not dared to
publicly own, Arabella languished alone in the
Tower for the last few years of her life. The
similarity in their fates—for both pined away
and died in captivity—is not the only point of
connection between them. Both were direct
descendants of Henry VII.; Arabella, the great-
granddaughter of Margaret Tudor, Queen of
Scotland, represented the elder branch, while
Katharine, though of an older generation, be-
longed to the younger one, being the grandchild
of Mary Tudor, Queen of France, and afterwards
Duchess of Suffolk. Curiously enough, also,
both ladies married into the same family, one

the son, the other the great-grandson, of the
Protector Somerset and his imperious duchess,
who boasted, we are told, of her descent from
five kings. To Edward Seymour, Katharine's
husband, the title of Earl of Hertford was given
by Elizabeth on her accession, while to his
grandson William, Arabella's husband, the title
of Duke of Somerset, taken from the Protector
on his fall, was restored more than a century later
by Charles II. Another strange coincidence
links their fates together. After the death of her
sister-in-law and sole confidant, Jane Seymour,
Katharine, left alone at court, her husband having
been ordered abroad, confided her story to one
Mistress Saintloe. This lady, when Countess
of Shrewsbury, afterwards got into trouble over
her daughter's marriage to Charles Stuart, Arabella's father. She received Katharine's unasked-
for intelligence with tears and sobs, knowing
full well that since Jane, the original culprit,
was no more, she would have to bear the whole
weight of the young bride's dangerous confi-
dence. And in truth poor Mistress Saintloe
was hurried off to the Tower as soon as the

queen discovered her knowledge of the affair.
Elizabeth may well have felt some pardonable
irritation when she found that Jane Seymour,
her trusted maid of honour, to whom she had
given a grand funeral in Westminster Abbey only
five months before, had been secretly employed
in "conspiring to shake her throne," as, in her
exaggerated fear and jealousy, the maiden queen
would have called her share in the marriage.

Whatever were Elizabeth's faults as a woman,
and they were indeed very serious, it must be
remembered that, as a queen, she needed all
her brilliant talents to consolidate a claim to
the English crown which might legally have
been disputed. Her father, Henry VIII., had
allowed his personal prejudices to override all
claims of birth and seniority. He had first repu-
diated his two daughters, Mary and Elizabeth,
for the shortcomings of their mothers, though
no sin save her failure to produce a male
heir, and her somewhat rigid Spanish character,
can be laid to poor Katharine of Arragon's
charge. Anne Boleyn's faults and frailties had
caused her little daughter Elizabeth to be, like

Mary, declared illegitimate, and thus their succession was made doubtful and difficult.

Fearful, perhaps, of the Scotch connection, and influenced by his personal preference for his younger sister Mary, Henry had also disinherited his elder sister Margaret, the Scotch queen, and her descendants, represented by James V. of Scotland, and his half-sister Margaret Douglas, Countess of Lenox, Arabella's paternal grandmother. On Henry's death, his niece Frances Brandon, Mary's daughter, who had married Henry Grey, Marquis of Dorset, was legally next heir to the crown after Edward VI., if Mary and Elizabeth were considered as debarred by their doubtful birthright from the succession, for they had been tardily restored to their rightful place in Henry's will before his death. Edward himself was, through Northumberland's influence, induced to sign a will, by which the crown passed to Jane Grey, her mother Frances voluntarily relinquishing her title. Thus we see that, on Jane's death, Katharine, her younger sister, was really perilously near the throne, and her marriage might prove of the utmost importance should Elizabeth die childless. But the fear was more present then than it can be to us nowadays, for we know that by the good sense of the English nation the superior claims of Margaret Tudor's descendants, the elder branch of the Stuarts, were finally preferred to that of the younger, and Elizabeth's fears proved groundless. Knowing this, however, we should take a more lenient view of the great queen's conduct in regard to her young relative, Arabella Stuart, sole female representative of the claims of the elder branch, and, should James die, her next heir. Other writers have blamed Elizabeth too much for her harsh treatment of Arabella. When the child was young, we shall find her received with every honour at court; but as she grew older, and her name became a centre for Catholic plots and ambitious schemes, the queen banished her from her presence; and when, just before her death, the rumour spread that Arabella was actually engaged to Katharine Grey's grandson, Elizabeth's wrath, strengthened most probably by remorse for her unkindness to Katharine, naturally blazed out, and Arabella was put under arrest.

Let us turn now to James, whose ultimate conduct admits of little palliation, resting, as it did, on a shadowy yet craven fear lest the united claims of the united branches of the Tudors should lose him his crown. He began, as was right and seemly, by treating his first cousin with the consideration due to her rank, and at first, in striking contrast to Elizabeth's later conduct, had Arabella always at court, paid her debts, and behaved to her in a proper and cousinly manner. But when the lady took the ill-advised step of wedding young William Seymour, James could not contain his fears, and hoped by imprisoning them both in separate prisons to avert the purely imaginary danger of their claims to the throne. James was not, like Elizabeth, childless; he had two sons to carry on his name and superior title to the succession —a title which neither Arabella nor Seymour could have disputed, nor, indeed, is there any evidence that they wished or intended to do so.

Before passing to the details of her life, it would be well to consider the character and appearance of Arabella, and attempt to place

her before our readers as she lived, though no
pen can do justice to charms which depended
so largely on a living, breathing presence. We
are told by Arabella's contemporaries of her
beauty; but it is difficult to see great beauty
in any of the portraits and miniatures which
have been handed down to us, though this is
—as in the case of the portraits of her aunt,
Mary Queen of Scots—no reason for doubting
the fact of her charms. The differences in all
the portraits are most confusing and baffling;
but when, as at the Stuart Exhibition, it was
possible to compare Arabella with some of her
relatives, it is not difficult to see how these differences arose. We are told, for instance, that
at the age of seven (see p. 59) she recalled her
handsome grandmother, the Countess of Lenox,
to Sir Walter Mildmay; and in the baby picture
of her (see No. 1),* the large, clear blue eyes
exactly resemble those in the miniatures of the
countess; while in the picture of Arabella when
a young girl (Nos. 2 and 3), the pursed-up
mouth is identical with that of her grandmother.

* In list of portraits, Part II., A, vol. ii. pp. 86–92.

The shape of her eyes, with their drooping lids, forcibly recalls her great-grandmother, Margaret Tudor, Queen of Scotland (see Holbein's portrait); but we must not forget that she bore also a likeness to her Stuart ancestry, more particularly in her last portrait (No. 5). But the Tudor influence certainly predominates. In Oliver's miniatures, and in one in particular, now in the possession of Mrs. Hogge, and reproduced by her kind permission in this volume, there is a slight resemblance to Elizabeth herself. It is possible, however, that the artist might have thought it his duty to flatter the young lady by accentuating her likeness to the Tudors, as, later on, when her last picture was taken, under James I., her resemblance to the Stuarts was accentuated, no doubt, for the same reason. The different colours given to her eyes are also most baffling—sometimes blue, sometimes brown; but the colour, a celestial blue, given her as a child, which became a gray blue, with yellow shades, as she grew older, and varied to hazel in some lights, is most generally considered to have been correct.

As to her hair, it was certainly not reddish, as some of the pictures represent it; the fashion in Elizabeth's days to dye the hair auburn like the queen's was followed by all ladies connected with the court, and as a young girl, before it was necessary to change the colour, Arabella's hair was light brown. So many and so fleeting, indeed, are all the likenesses traced in Arabella's numerous portraits, that one may see resemblances to all and each of her principal relations, including the Cavendishes. The sweet child clutching a doll, dressed like herself in the stiff costume of the period, grew at the ungraceful age of thirteen or fourteen into a plain girl; and since while she was in her teens Arabella was a more important personage than in her later life, the greater number of her pictures and miniatures represent her in the plain stage. Some of Isaac Oliver's miniatures (especially one taken about the age of eighteen or nineteen, with hair done up, belonging to General Sotheby) are the most attractive, and give one some idea of her appearance in the bloom of her youth. There is afterwards a long gap, till the last portrait (No. 5), taken of her when at James's court, shows us a rather severe-looking but handsome lady, " the most learned Lady Arbella," as she used to be called ; and she had, indeed, a claim to that title. Books were always her chief solace. She would often escape from the frivolous court in Anne of Denmark's days to her books ; and, in the disgrace of 1603, one of her grievances is that she is shut out from her study-chamber where her dear dead friends live. French and Italian she knew and spoke ; Latin and Greek were familiar tongues to her, especially the former ; her letters are full of quotations from the classics ; and we give in the Second Part two Latin notes, which she wrote with her own hand, as specimens of her scholarship.

Mary Queen of Scots, as if aware of her niece's tastes even at her then early age, left her in her will an illuminated Book of Hours. This is a most interesting volume, not only in its beautiful binding and illuminations, but also because it contains signatures of many notable persons. Mary first had the book in France

(it is written in French), and on the twelfth page
she wrote herself, " Ce livre est à moy Marie
Reyne, 1554." These words are the only ones
written in France ; the rest of the autographs,
either verses by herself or names of her friends,
belong to the time of her captivity. Several
names were written after the book passed into
Arabella's possession. Amongst others it is
interesting to note those of the old Countess of
Shrewsbury, Francis Bacon, and the Earl of
Nottingham. Arabella wrote her own name
after her marriage and during her captivity,
"Your most unfortunat Arbella Seymour," and
it is permissible to conjecture that the precious
book may have been sent as a token to her
husband, for it certainly got taken to Paris in
the seventeenth century. It was there pur-
chased during the Revolution, and carried to
St. Petersburg, where it may now be seen in the
Musée de l'Ermitage.

Arabella herself did full justice in after-life to
the careful education she received while under
the care of her maternal grandmother. But it
was not only her appearance and her attainments

which called forth the admiration of her contemporaries. Her friends were many, and she
was also beloved by her servants and depen-
dants, as even the unhappy chaplain, who hanged
himself on account, ostensibly, of her neglect to
help him to a benefice, if for no tenderer reason,
testifies in his dying confession. The ridiculous
William Fowler (see p. 174) was certainly half in
love with her, and falls into rhapsodies over her
appearance and virtues. But she was not all
goodness and virtues. She loved, in her youth
especially, to thwart her guardians, and even her
sovereign ; her wilfulness is a constant source
of worry to her grandmother, and by all accounts
she must have been a most headstrong young
woman. She was wont also to be carried away
by her feelings, a creature of impulse and whims,
perhaps all the more fascinating to those who
loved her for that reason. Her uncle Gilbert,
Earl of Shrewsbury, and his wife Mary, were,
in spite of occasional misunderstandings, from
her earliest childhood, her firm friends, and her
letters to them are far the most natural and
charming in her whole correspondence, and filled

with the bright flashes of her gay humour. Throughout the strange and somewhat hysterical letters of that troublous time when she was struggling to escape from her old grandmother (1603), Arabella seems always laughing in her sleeve, and we are quite prepared for the brilliancy of her humour in her correspondence when fortune smiled on her. Religious she no doubt was, and, we are told, fond of listening to sermons; she constantly speaks of herself as a Puritan, a kind of protestation against the perpetual attempts of the Jesuits, during her earlier years, to convert her. These attempts were all in vain, for Arabella was, and remained all through her life, a firm Protestant.

That gay humour of hers was required to bear her up throughout the constant troubles of her stormy life, and she needed the help of the adage which is inscribed on a jewel that hangs round her neck in her earliest portrait, " Pour Parvenir j'endure." This motto was, indeed, fated to be hers through life, and must often have been her strength and solace when the clouds of misfortune gathered round her.

CHAPTER II.

PARENTAGE, BIRTH, AND INFANCY.

1574–1580.

WE have dwelt at some length upon the appearance and character of our heroine; let us now, stone by stone, build up her story, from the too scanty materials which our own labour and the researches of others in the same field have been able hitherto to discover.

The corner-stone of every biography is the birth and parentage of its subject. Arabella's connection * with the royal family has been referred to; it is now time to turn to the lives and fortunes of her immediate progenitors. Her father's mother, Margaret Douglas, to whom Arabella bore a strong family resemblance, began life in a fortress on the Scotch border, where her

* See Genealogy, Part II., vol. ii. p. 85.

mother, Margaret Tudor, the ex-Queen of Scots, then the wife of Douglas, Earl of Angus, had taken refuge from her own subjects.

After a girlhood spent at her rough father's side, and early separated from her mother, Margaret had a brief triumph in the sun of royal favour. Beautiful even at fifty, in her teens she was admired by all, and the first misfortune of her life was the too fervent adoration of a youthful gallant, Lord Thomas Howard. The foolish young couple, encouraged, as they thought, by the smiles of Henry and his giddy consort, Anne Boleyn, went so far as a solemn but secret betrothal, possibly even a marriage; but the sudden downfall of Howard's relative, the queen, destroyed their hopes of royal favour. Before long the king heard of their fault, and they were both imprisoned in the Tower, whence Margaret, falling ill, was soon removed to custody in the country, but where poor Howard pined away and died of prison fever. Such was the tragic end of Margaret's first and only romance; but she was destined to be a happy wife. Seven years after

her lover's death and her own restoration to
court favour, a political union was arranged
for her by her royal uncle, and at the age
of twenty-nine she married Matthew Stuart,
Earl of Lenox. Though purely a *mariage de
convenance*, and not one of inclination, Margaret and her husband became very much
attached to one another, and throughout the
troubles of their later life their mutual affection never wavered for an instant. The earl
writes affectionately of and to his "sweet
Mage;" and when, in 1561–2, he was incar-
cerated in the Tower, on suspicion of planning
a match between his elder son Darnley and
Mary Queen of Scots, his wife wrote constant
letters to Cecil and others interceding for his
release, and representing the bad effect of the
close confinement on his health. Margaret was
not allowed to share his imprisonment; but
at last he was released from the Tower, and
sent to join her and her son Charles, then
about five, and another child (who afterwards
died) at Sheen, where, since their disgrace,
Margaret had lived in the custody of Sir

Richard and Lady Sackville. The winter of
1562 was spent at Sheen, where the earl was
very ill; but at last, in February, 1563, they
and their children were allowed to go free,
though they refused to consider themselves
restored to favour till they were permitted to
see the queen " face to face." This was not
granted; their offence, they were told, was
forgiven and forgotten, yet Elizabeth would
not see them, and, crippled by the debts
incurred by their ruinous imprisonment, they
retired to their Yorkshire estate of Settrington
to retrieve their fallen fortunes.

Margaret remained there for the next two
years, while her husband and eldest son went
off to Scotland, determined, in spite of the earl's
experience of the Tower, to carry on the young
man's marriage to the Scotch queen. For
this rash union Margaret had to suffer, by
being sent to the Tower in 1565, while the earl
and Darnley were safe from Elizabeth's wrath
at Edinburgh.

With young Charles, Arabella's father, we
have more concern than with his feeble

dissolute brother, and in the State Papers there is a minute from Queen Elizabeth, dated September 1, 1565,* directing one Charles Vaughan and his wife, Lady Knevet, to go to Settrington and take charge of the boy, "being of tender years" (he was nine years old), and to take special care of his health and safety.

After the murder of Darnley, the earl and his wife, by their importunate cries for vengeance on the murderer, were again restored to favour, the countess released from custody, and they were allowed to return to Settrington, where the little Charles was given back to his mother's keeping.

When Mary fled to Elizabeth's protection, the Lenoxes hastened to court, and in deepest mourning knelt before the queen, the lady's face swelled and stained with tears as she cried so passionately for vengeance, that at last Elizabeth thought it right to reprove her for her vehemence†; while the earl opened the Commission of Enquiry at Westminster by a speech, in which he also appealed for revenge.

* State Papers, Eliz., Dom., vol. xxxvii. p. 25, MS.
† Udall's "Life of Mary Queen of Scots.'

Nothing came of their appeals, but in 1570 Margaret was completely restored to Elizabeth's favour, and made her first lady, while the earl was sent, as regent, to Scotland. This honour proved, however, disastrous to him, for in the autumn of 1571 he was assassinated at Stirling. His disconsolate widow was thus left in sole charge of her last remaining son, Charles, now at the troublesome age of fifteen, and she seems to have found the boy very difficult to manage.

Barely two months (November 4) after her husband's death, she writes * from her house at Islington to her constant friend Burghley, to express the anxiety and vexation she sustains in bringing up her only son ; instead of being her greatest comfort, he was her "greatest dolour."

She desires to "bewraye" unto the lord-treasurer "a special grief which long time and chiefly of late hath grown upon me through the bringing up of my only son Charles. . . . And having awakened myself lately [from her

* State Papers, Eliz., Dom., 1571, vol. lxxxiii. p. 5, MS.

grief], I have found that his father's absence so long time in his riper years hath made lack to be to him in divers ways that were answerable in his brother. . . . And though the good hap of this [Charles] hath not been to have that help of the father's company that his brother had, whereby at these years he is somewhat unfurnished of qualities needful, and I, being now a lone woman, am less able to have him well reformed at home than before," yet the special care she has that he might be able to continue a worthy memory of his father's house, and serve his prince and country, leads her to ask Burghley to take him into his house.

If Charles in any way resembled his weak and obstinate brother Darnley, poor Margaret had good cause to complain ; but there is nothing to show the real character of the boy, except his tutor's favourable account of him, which we shall see later on. The countess's own leaning to the Romish Church was one cause of her perpetual trouble, and now the queen, through Burghley, desired that her son should be brought up a Protestant.

Accordingly, one of the friends of Bullinger and other Reformers, Malliet by name, became, in the spring of the next year, Charles's preceptor, and gives the following account of him: "I went to England," he says—in a letter * dated May 26, 1572, from Gray's Inn, to Bullinger the younger—"where I undertook the office of tutor and governor to the Earl of Lenox, the brother of the King of Scots who was murdered, and uncle to the present one, not without a great deal of trouble and hindrance to my studies. But induced by the entreaties and promises of the principal personages of this kingdom, I could not decline to take that burden for a limited time, since I am at full liberty to leave this place whenever I choose. The youth is just entering on his sixteenth year, and gives great promise of hope for the future. For in case the present king, his nephew, should die without lawful issue, he is the sole successor by hereditary right to the crown of Scotland, and is entitled to be placed at the head of the kingdom and empire.

* Zürich Letters, 2nd series, p. 200.

So also no one is more nearly allied to the royal blood of England, after the death of the present queen, than his mother, to whom her only son is heir; although there is now being held an assembly of all the states of the realm (which in common language is called a Parliament) to the end that an undisputed heir to the throne may be appointed by the general consent of all parties, lest, in case hereafter of the queen's death, any disturbance should arise."

As a matter of fact, Malliet's confident assertion that the question of the succession was about to be decided proved a vain one, and much of the troubles of the realm were to come from the perpetual doubt and perplexity caused by the queen's obstinate refusal to allow this vexed question to be finally settled. Until Charles was eighteen he continued to live with his mother, and under Malliet's teaching, at her house at Hackney, whither she had removed from Islington. All was now well with the countess, and she was allowed to visit the queen from time to time; but troubles were brewing which were again to give the unfortunate lady a taste of prison walls.

The Queen of Scots was now under the charge of the Earl of Shrewsbury at Sheffield and Chatsworth, and Margaret, who seems by this time to have forgiven, or, for policy, forgotten, her once furious denunciation of her daughter-in-law, was suspected by Elizabeth of consulting with her about a bride for young Charles. Whatever the truth of this, and whether premeditated or not, it is certain that the bride ultimately selected proved to be the step-daughter of Mary's gaoler, and therefore one with whom the captive queen had an intimate acquaintance. We have spoken of Shrewsbury's countess, Elizabeth, in connection with Katharine Grey's imprisonment. She was then Mistress Saintloe, but since that time she had wedded a fourth husband. By her second and "most dear and well-beloved"— as, with scant courtesy to her first (Mr. Barlow), she calls Sir William Cavendish—she had eight children ; and her fourth, George Talbot, Earl of Shrewsbury, had already a flourishing family by a former wife, so that the Cavendishes and Talbots perpetually strove for the mastery in the poor old earl's house. The countess herself—"Bess of Hardwick," as she is familiarly called—was a lady of indomitable temper, and as strong a character as Margaret of Lenox ; and both ambitious mothers, seeing the advantage of a union between their families, the riches being on the Cavendish side, and the high rank on the Stuart, no doubt deliberately planned the meeting which took place, ostensibly by chance, between Charles Stuart and Elizabeth Cavendish.

On October 9, 1574, the Countess of Lenox and her son left London, bound, so she took care to publish abroad, for Settrington, and thence to Scotland, to see her grandchild, James VI. On their way northwards they rested for a few days at Huntingdon, with the charming Katharine, Countess of Suffolk, widow of Charles Brandon, and now wife of Mr. Bertie. The Countess of Shrewsbury happened, of course by accident, to be at Rufford, one of her numerous country seats, close by, and, taking her fair young daughter with her, she hastened over to Huntingdon, and insisted on the travellers coming to stay a few days with her. Rufford being "not one mile distant out of my way," as Margaret explains in her letter * of excuse to Leicester, "yea, and a much fairer way, as is well to be proved, and my lady meeting me herself upon the way, I could not refuse it, being near thirty miles from Sheffield."

Before leaving London, it seems that the queen had sent for Margaret, and at the end of their conversation had, in answer to a question if she might go to Chatsworth, another of the Shrewsburys' seats, where Mary Queen of Scots was kept when not at Sheffield, refused her consent, lest she should be suspected of agreeing with her daughter-in-law; but Rufford being so far from Derbyshire, the countess saw no harm in going there. Whether by chance or arrangement, Margaret fell ill, and, "being sickly, . . . rested her at Rufford five days, and kept most her bedchamber." †

* State Papers, Eliz., Dom., December, 1574, vol. xcix. p. 12 (1), MS.
† See Shrewsbury's letter on next page.

During this short time matters were so cleverly arranged by the wily hostess that, before his mother was able to continue her journey, Charles had fallen desperately in love with Elizabeth Cavendish, and so entangled himself, his mother affirms in the same letter to Leicester, that he could have none other bride. In a letter dated from Sheffield, November 5, 1574, from the girl's step-father, the Earl of Shrewsbury, to Leicester, we read that the young people "hath so tied themselves upon their own liking as cannot part. My wife hath sent him to my lady [of Lenox], and the young man is so far in love that belike he is sick without her." He pathetically adds that he shall be well at quiet if the match comes off, since "there is few noblemen's sons in England that she [his wife] hath not prayed me to deal for at one time or other. . . . And now this comes unlooked for, without thanks to me." *

No obstacle being raised by the countess to her son's choice, their problematic journey north-

* " Howard Collection of Letters," pp. 235–237.

wards was now openly abandoned, and the marriage hastened on with all possible speed —in fact, with indecent haste, lest the queen should interfere with the project. Only a few weeks at most can have passed from the lovers' first acquaintance to the marriage ceremony; for it must have been celebrated in the end of October or the beginning of November, certainly before November 17, since on that day the queen, having heard of what had taken place, sent messengers to summon all those concerned in arranging the match to London, with threats of imprisonment, and violent words expressive of her wrath. The two ladies and the bridal pair were therefore obliged, towards the end of the month, to set off for the court, but as the country was under water from the wet November weather, their progress was extremely slow.

Meantime the earl hastened to clear himself from any complicity in the affair, though, as we have seen, he had already most unwisely expressed his joy at getting one of his stepchildren off his hands. On December 2 he writes * from Sheffield, where he remained in charge of his state prisoner, to Burghley and Leicester, "concerning the marriage of my lady daughter."

"I must confess to your Majesty," says the poor man, full of anxiety to exculpate himself at the expense of his troublesome, ambitious wife, " as true it is, that it was dealt in suddenly, and without my knowledge ; but as I dare undertake and insure [assure] to your Majesty, for my wife, she finding her daughter disappointed of young Barté, where she hoped, and that other young gentleman was inclined to love with a few days' acquaintance, did her best to further her daughter to this match, without having therein any other intent or respect than with reverent duty towards your Majesty she ought. I wrote of this matter to my Lord of Leicester a good while ago, at great length. I hid nothing from him that I knew was done about the same ; and thought not meet to trouble your Majesty therewith, because I took it to be of no such importance

* Lodge, "Illustrations of British History," vol. ii. p. 122.

as to write of, until now that I am urged by such as I see will not forbear to devise and speak what may procure any suspicion or doubtfulness of my service here."

On December 3 there was much excitement in high quarters caused by the non-arrival of the Countess of Lenox, and some anxiety was expressed as to her movements.* The poor lady was, however, detained by no fault of her own at Huntingdon, whence she writes to Burghley and Leicester, explaining that her delay was caused by "the great unquietness and trouble that I have had with passing these dangerous waters, which hath many times enforced me to leave my way . . . and being forced to stay this present Friday in Huntingdon, somewhat to refresh myself and my overlaboured mules, that are both crooked and lame with their extreme labour by the way, I thought good to lay open to your lordship [Leicester] in these few lines what I have to say for [me]." Then follow the excuses we have given above (p. 26) from this same letter, and she implores

* Calendar of State Papers, Eliz., Dom., 1574, p. 489.

both noblemen to intercede for her with the queen.

It was not till the second week in December that Margaret reached London; she was at Hackney on the 10th,† and on the 12th the French ambassador reports to Henry III. that she came to court. "She fears greatly the indignation of Queen Elizabeth her mistress, and that she will send her to the Tower on account of the marriage of her son. Still, she relies on friends, whom she hopes will save her from this blow."

Elizabeth's wrath was terrible when roused, but at first she was content to order all the culprits to remain in their own houses, and speak only with those whom the Privy Council allowed them to see. We have referred to the suspected complicity of Mary Queen of Scots, and it was evident that the queen's anger was caused, not so much by a marriage undertaken without her consent—which, it is true, was generally enough for her—as by the fear of a reconciliation between Mary and her mother-

* Calendar of State Papers, Eliz., Dom., 1574, p. 489.

in-law, who had been at deadly feud since
Darnley's murder.   There seems, indeed, reason
to believe in the truth (p. 41) of an understanding having lately been arrived at by the
two sworn foes, and we shall afterwards find
the Scotch queen taking much interest in the
offspring of a match which she was thought to
have helped to bring about.*

The Earl of Shrewsbury, after having by
Lady Lenox's "earnest request" written to the
Lords of the Council on her behalf, refers to
this rumour in a letter † to Lord Burghley of
December 27 : "I do not nor can," he says,
"find the marriage of that lady's son to my
wife's daughter can any way be taken, with
indifferent [impartial] judgment, to be any
offence or contemptuous to her Majesty ; and
then methinks that benefit any subject may by
law claim might be permitted to any of mine
as well.   But I must be plain with your lordship.   It is not the marriage matter, nor the
hatred some bear to my Lady Lenox, my wife,

* Udall's "Life of Mary Queen of Scots," pp. 242, 246.
† Lodge, "Illustrations of British History," vol. ii. p. 126.

or to me, that makes this great ado, and occupies heads with so many devises : it is *a greater matter*, which I leave to conjecture, not doubting but your lordship's wisdom hath foreseen it, and thereof had due consideration, as always you have been most careful for it."

Soon after Christmas both the countesses had been lodged in the Tower, whither also Charles's tutor had been sent ; but he and his bride were allowed to retire to (probably) Chatsworth, another of his mother-in-law's country seats. There they seem to have spent the spring and summer, and there, in the late summer or early autumn of 1575, their only child was born. The place is settled by two pedigrees found in the Harleian MSS. Though in one an incorrect date (1548) is given for the birth of Charles himself, both pedigrees * agree in Arabella's birthplace, " Nata 1575, apud Chatsworth, in Anglia," and, "Born at Chatsworth, 1575." The child was baptized by the name of Arbella (so spelt and pronounced in

* Harl. MSS., 588, fols. 13 and 23 ; Miss Cooper's "Life of Arabella Stuart," vol. i. p. 37 ; Hunter's "Hallamshire," p. 92.

those days), probably in the parish church close by, Edensor; but no record of her baptism remains. We only know that one of her mother's own brothers, Charles, stood godfather, the other sponsors being her mother's sister, Mary Cavendish, and her husband, Gilbert Talbot, the second son by a former wife of the old Earl of Shrewsbury. Gilbert and his wife were Arabella's guardians throughout her life, and her aunt Mary supplied in part the place of her mother later on.

Meantime the Commission, under the Earl of Huntingdon, appointed to examine into the accusations against Margaret of Lenox, the chief culprit, dragged slowly on. Her most trusted friend and servant, Thomas Fowler, and all her household were examined, but nothing could be elicited, and finally both countesses were suffered to return to their homes—Bess being back at Sheffield with her husband by March. The exact date of Margaret's release is uncertain; by the winter of 1575, however, she was back at Hackney, where her son, his wife and *infant* (unless the pedigrees are wrong, and Arabella was born at Hackney), had joined her before November 10 ; and there they all lived together for the present.

That Mary Queen of Scots already took an interest in the baby heiress of the house of Lenox, and also that she was now outwardly on good terms with her mother-in-law, may be seen by a letter * which Margaret wrote her on November 10, thanking her for her "good re-membrance and bounty to our little daughter here, who some day may serve your Highness," and signing herself, "Your Majesty's most humble and loving mother and aunt." Between the date and the signature is a postscript by Arabella's mother, in which she humbly thanks the captive queen for remembering her poor servant (herself), " both with a token, and in my lady's gracious letter " (a letter Mary had written to the countess). She also represents herself as ready to do her Majesty's service as any servant she has, " according as by duty I am bound. I beseech your Highness to pardon

* State Papers, Scottish Series, Mary Queen of Scots, vol. x. p. 71, MS.

these rude lines, and accept the good heart of the writer, who loves and honours your Majesty unfeignedly."

Before her marriage, Elizabeth Cavendish must have had many opportunities of seeing her step-father's prisoner, and had evidently felt, like all who approached her, the charms and fascination of Mary Stuart, now her sister-in-law.

As for Mary's baby-niece, Arabella, she was never destined to be, according to her grand-mother's hopes, of service to the captive queen ; her own fate was rather to be decided in after-years by Mary's son, her cousin James. Even now misfortunes were crowding round her unconscious head. Before she was two years old, and before the sweet baby-picture of her at twenty-three months was painted, her young father died of rapid consumption (early in April, 1576). The earldom and lands of Lenox had been granted by James, soon after Matthew Stuart's death (in April, 1572), to Charles Stuart and his heirs for ever, with the consent of the Regent Mar and the nobility and

Council.* On the young earl's death, a question was at once raised about the title of his heiress ; and James sheltered himself, being still a minor, behind the late lord regent (Earl of Mar), giving his successor, Lord Morton, the unpleasant task of disinheriting the fatherless child. The regent (Morton), "being requested to grant the wardship of the lands unto Elizabeth, Countess of Lenox, for her dower, not only denied the same, but also denied to allow the Lady Arabella as heir to the earldom. So that the regent will not permit the countess to deal with the said earldom neither in her own right as her dower, nor in the right of the young lady as tutor or guardian unto her." †

The child's grandmother wrote ‡ on April 24, 1576, to Lord Ruthven, the first letter she says she had written since her son's death, asking for information about the earldom of Lenox, and whether it is heritable by his daughter.

* Harl. MSS., 289, fol. 196 (from original). See Ellis's "Letters," 2nd series, vol. ii. p. 58.
† Ibid.
‡ State Papers, Scottish Series, Elizabeth, vol. xxvii. p. 5, MS.

In the following year, however, she had quite
made up her mind on the subject, as appears by
her statement of her dower,* "the right heiress"
being Arabella. The quarrel was destined to
drag on till the old countess had passed away
from the sordid cares which darkened her last
years. It was in vain that Elizabeth and Lord
Burghley took up the cudgels on the poor
little heiress's behalf; the regent was ready
with objections. He declared † that not only
had the earldom fallen into the king's hands
by reason of ward on Charles's death, ·and
that till the age of eighteen Arabella's claims
could not be considered, but also that any gift
made by the regent in the king's minority might
"be revoked [by the sovereign] at any time,
either within age or at full age."

Mary Queen of Scots had interested herself
on Arabella's side of the question. Just before
Charles's death, in an unfinished will, she had
nominated him or Lord Claud Hamilton, in
case of James's decease, to the Scotch succes-

* Calendar of State Papers, Scottish Series, Eliz., p. 395.
† Harl. MSS., 289, fols. 200, 202.

sion, also restoring to old Lady Lenox "all the rights she can pretend to the earldom of Angus." By the time the will was completed Charles had died, and Mary therefore added a clause, giving "to my niece Arbella the earldom of Lenox, held by her late father, and enjoin my son, as my heir and successor, to obey my will in this particular."

As we shall see, James had no intention of obeying his mother's wishes, " in this particular " at any rate. At this time Arabella lost another protector, under whose roof her babyhood had been passed. In the very heat of the controversy about her grandchild's inheritance, the old Countess Dowager of Lenox, "having survived eight children," worn out by perpetual struggles with sorrow and poverty, and over-burdened with debts, died at Hackney, March 9, 1578. This is no place to discuss her faults, chiefly those of a fiery and high-spirited nature ; let us rather turn to Camden's account * of her.

* "Annals," p. 227. Udall, in his " Life of Mary Queen of Scots," sums up Margaret's character in much the same words, and repeats her account of her imprisonments (p. 216).

"She was a matron of singular piety, patience, and modesty," he says, "who was thrice cast into the Tower (as I have heard her say herself), not for any crime of treason, but for love matters; first when Thomas Howard, son of the first Duke of Norfolk of that name, falling in love with her, died in the Tower of London; then for the love of Henry, Lord Darnley, her son, to Mary Queen of Scots; and lastly for the love of Charles her younger son to Elizabeth Cavendish, mother to the Lady Arbella, with whom the Queen of Scots was accused to have made up the match."

To atone, perhaps, for her former unkindness, and also to avoid the disgrace of a pauper funeral —for the old countess left no money for her burial—Elizabeth caused her to be laid with much pomp in a vault in the Chapel of Henry VII., and defrayed the charges of a stately funeral, Clarencieux the herald attending to proclaim the deceased lady's titles, and every honour as to a relative of the royal family being paid to her remains, which had been scantily given to her in life. A beautiful altar tomb, on which Margaret's alabaster effigy reposes after all the strife and turmoil of her life, was raised over her grave. Round it kneel her children. Darnley, with a broken crown above his head, comes first; then Charles, whose body is said to lie in the vault below, placed there two years before his mother's. So poor did the countess die that the only legacy in her power to leave her granddaughter was a casket of jewels,* which she gave to her confidential servant, Thomas Fowler, to be handed over to Arabella when she reached the age of fourteen.

With her daughter-in-law, Mary Stuart, the old countess died at peace. About a month (May 2) after Margaret's death, the Scotch queen wrote † to the Archbishop of Glasgow, to say that she had been "in good correspondence" for some five or six years with the countess, who "has confessed to me in her own handwriting, which I keep, the injury which she did me by unjust accusations." Arabella is, she

---

* See list in State Papers, Eliz., Dom., vol. ccxxxi. p. 99, MS.
† Tytler's "Enquiry," vol. ii. p. 70.

says, in Queen Elizabeth's care, and Mary has
written to those about her son to enter a claim
for the Lenox lands in his name.

But Matthew Stuart's English lands had long
been seized upon by the Crown, and now, when
Elizabeth might gracefully have yielded them
to the poverty-stricken heiress, she not only
denied James's rights to them—which were, of
course, superior to his cousin's—but "would not
give ear to those who affirmed that the Lady
Arbella, daughter to Charles, the king's uncle,
and born in England, was next heir to the
lands in England." She therefore commanded
the English estates "to be sequestered, and
signified to the [Scotch] ambassador that James
should pay his grandmother's creditors out of
the Scotch lands. For she took it not well that
the king, after the death of Charles his uncle,
had revoked the infeoffment of the earldom of
Lenox made to his uncle and his heirs for
ever, and that to the prejudice (as was suggested) of the Lady Arbella, though by the
privilege of the Scots it was still lawful for
them to revoke all such grants and donations

as were prejudicial to the realm and made in their minority." *   That Lord Burghley exerted himself on Arabella's behalf in the question of the Scotch inheritance, we see by the following grateful letter † from Elizabeth Lenox— one of the very few remains of Arabella's mother :—

"I can but yield your lordship most hearty thanks for your continual goodness towards me and my little one, and specially for your lordship's late good dealing with the Scots' ambassador for my poor child's right, for which, as also sundry other ways, we are for ever bound to your lordship, whom I beseech still to further that cause as to your lordship may seem best. I can assure your lordship the earldom of Lenox was granted by Act of Parliament to my lord, my late husband, and the heirs of his body, so that they should offer great wrong in seeking to take it from *Arbela ;* which I trust by your lordship's good means will be pre-

---

* Ellis's "Letters," 2nd series, vol. ii. p. 461.

† Lansd. MSS., 27, art. 5, from original ; printed in Ellis's "Letters," 2nd series, vol. ii. p. 57.

vented, being of your mere goodness for justice'
sake, so well disposed therunto. For all which
your lordship's goodness (as I am bound) I rest
in heart more thankful than I can anyways
express. I take my leave of your lordship,
whom I pray God long to preserve.

"At Newgate Street, the xv. of August [1578].

"Your lordship, as I am bounden,

"E. LENOX.

"Upon my advertisement to my lady, my
mother, of the infection at Chelsey (from whence
I would at the first have removed if I had
known any fit place), though the danger was
not great, she hath commanded me presently to
come hither for want of a more convenient
house."

Leicester also took some trouble to see justice
done to the fatherless child ; and Lady Lenox
wrote to him* on August 25, to express her
gratitude for his good offices "in the just cause
of my poor infant for the earldom of Lenox."
At last, no doubt through the representations

* "Howard Collection of Letters," p. 363.

and influence of these two powerful favourites, the queen compromised for having seized the English lands (which seem, after all, to have been granted by Henry VIII. to Matthew Lenox and his heirs *male*, and were therefore legally the Scotch king's birthright), by granting the young Countess of Lenox a life pension of £400 a year, and £200 to the child—£600 in all.* The queen has been accused of parsimony in this matter, but it should be remembered that the sum of £600 equals a much larger amount nowadays—about five times the present value; and, since the widow and daughter now resided entirely with the wealthy old Countess of Shrewsbury, they were very comfortably provided for.

James had meantime finally snatched away the earldom of Lenox; though on her portrait, taken some years later, after her mother's death, Arabella is wrongfully called Countess of Lenox. The Scotch king granted both title and lands (June 16, 1578) to Robert, Earl of Caithness (uncle to Charles Stuart), who resigned it in

* Ellis, "Letters," 2nd series, vol. ii. p. 58.

1581 * to James's relative and favourite, Esmé
Stuart, Lord d'Aubigny.   At the same time,
however, and as if to atone for his robbery,
James suggested that Arabella's claims should
be settled and compromised by her marriage
with Esmé—a proposal renewed some years
later, but which was again indignantly refused
by Elizabeth.

* Douglas, " Peerage of Scotland," vol. ii. pp. 98, 99.

CHAPTER III.

1582-1590.

WHEN Arabella was between six and seven she lost her young mother. Elizabeth Stuart died at Sheffield Manor (Sunday, January 21, 1581–2), at which place and at Chatsworth she had lived since her mother-in-law's death, and where she and Arabella must often have been in the society of the imprisoned Queen of Scotland. The Earl of Shrewsbury writes* on the same day (January 21) to Burghley and Leicester, to announce his step-daughter's death, saying she made a "most goodlie and goode ende. Sundry times," he continues, "did she make her most earnest and humble prayer to the Almighty for her Majesty's most happy estate, and the long

* Lansd. MSS., 34, fol. 1, from original; printed in Ellis's "Letters," 2nd series, vol. iii. p. 60.

and prosperous continuance thereof, and, as one
most infinitely bound to her Highness, humbly
and lowly beseeched her Majesty to have pity
upon her poor orphaned *Arbella Stewarde;* and,
as at all times heretofore, both the mother and
poor daughter was most infinitely bound to her
Highness, so her assured trust was that her
Majesty would continue the same accustomed
goodness and bounty to the poor child she left.
With her last breath she begged that this petition might be presented to the queen, and a
'poor remembrance' will shortly be sent to her
Majesty by her wish. My wife," concludes the
earl, "taketh my daughter Lenox's death so
grievously that she neither doth nor can think
of anything but of lamenting and weeping."

He writes * at the same time to the same
effect to Sir Francis Walsingham, "to whom my
daughter in her life, and her infant the Lady
Arbella Stuart, hath been very much bound. I
pray you so now after her death be you a mean
to her Majesty to present my daughter Lenox's
humble and lowly thanks to her Majesty,

* State Papers, Eliz., Dom., vol. clii. fol. 9, MS.

with her prayer for the long and happy estate of her Majesty." Again he dwells upon the great grief his wife, who "cannot think of aught but tears," is enduring. But a week later Bess had recovered sufficiently to think of temporal affairs; and on the 28th of the month she writes to Walsingham and Burghley, to secure that Elizabeth's pension might be continued with her own £200 to the orphan. To both she expresses herself willing to submit to the Divine will in the loss of her daughter; and to Walsingham she dwells cunningly on the argument that she needs the money "to go to the child for her better education, and training up in all good virtue and learning, and so she may the sooner be ready to attend on her Majesty." She asks leave from both lords that William Cavendish, her favourite and second son, may attend on them to know their "good pleasure in this matter."

Her letter * to Lord Burghley is warmer in tone than that to Walsingham. After the pre-

---

* Lansd. MSS., 34, art. 2, from original; printed in Ellis's "Letters," 2nd series, vol. ii. p. 62.

face about her loss, she says, " I shall not need
here to make long recital to your lordship how
that in all my greatest matters I have been
singularly bound to your lordship for your
lordship's good and especial favour to me ; and
how much your lordship did bind me, the poor
woman that is gone, and my sweet juell Arbella
at our last being at court, neither the mother
during her life nor I can ever forget, but most
thankfully acknowledge it ; and so I am well
assured will the young babe when her riper
years will suffer her to know her best friends.
And now, my good lord, I hope her Majesty,
upon my most humble suit, will let that portion
which her Majesty bestowed on my daughter,
and juell Arbella, remain wholly to the child
for her better education. Her servants that are
to look to her, her masters that are to train her
up in all good learning and virtue, will require
no small charges."

Receiving no satisfactory answer to her pe-
tition, the old countess, a few months later
(May 6, 1582), again wrote to both ministers,
Burghley and Walsingham, using this time

the dangerous argument of her grandchild's re-
lationship to the queen, to induce her to grant
the whole £600. Both letters are interesting, as
they show that, though no doubt her motives
were prompted by self-interest, the grandmother
took real trouble about the education of the
child. She dwells again on her grief for her
daughter's death, "whom it pleased God," she
says* to Lord Burghley, "(I doubt not in mercy
for her good, but to my no small grief, in her
best time), to take out of this world, whom I
cannot yet remember but with a sorrowful,
troubled mind. I am now, my good lord, to be
an humble suitor to the queen's Majesty, that
it may please her to confirm that grant of the
whole £600 yearly for the education of my
dearest jewel Arbella, wherein I assuredly
trust to her Majesty's most gracious goodness,
who never denied me any suit. . . . And as I
know your lordship hath especial care for the
ordering of her Majesty's revenues, and of her
estate every way, so trust I you will consider

* Lansd. MSS., 34, p. 143, from original ; printed in Ellis's
" Letters," 2nd series, vol. iii. p. 64.

of the poor infant's case, who, under her Majesty, is to appeal only unto your lordship for succour in her distresses ; who, I trust, cannot dislike of this my suit in her behalf, considering the charges incident to her bringing up. For although she were ever where her mother was during her life, yet can I not now like she should be here, nor in any place else, where I may not sometimes see her, and daily hear of her, and therefore charged with keeping house where she must be with such as is fit for her calling, of whom I have special care, not only such as a natural mother hath of her best beloved child, but much more greater *in respect how she is in blood to her Majesty*, albeit one of the poorest, as depending wholly of her Majesty's gracious bounty and goodness, and being now upon vii. years, and very apt to learn and able to conceive what shall be taught. The charge will so increase, as I doubt not her Majesty will well conceive the six hundred pounds yearly to be little enough, which, as your lordship knoweth, is but as so much in money, for that the lands be in lease, and no

further commodity to be looked for during these
few years of the child's minority."

The estates referred to are probably some
lands which Arabella inherited as her mother's
share of the Cavendish heritage, or possibly
an estate of Margaret Lenox's, called Smallwood, belonging to Arabella, about which law-
suits were held at various times. She may, however, mean that a petition the earl sent in on
Elizabeth's behalf just before her death, asking
that the countess may have " in farm " the old
Countess of Lenox's lands, paying rent to the
queen, was acceded to, and that Arabella only
rented her grandmother's lands from the Crown.
The *naïveté* of Bess of Hardwick's arguments
is delightful, and she repeats much the same in
her letter,* written on the same day (May 6)
to Walsingham. She says again that Arabella
" being near well towards seven years old, she
is of very great towardness to learn anything,
and I very careful of her good education, as if
she were my own and only child, and a great
deal more for the consanguinity she is of to her

* State Papers, Eliz., Dom., vol. cliii. p. 39, MS.

Majesty." However, by another letter she writes
in January, 1583, the queen seems to have turned
a deaf ear to her moving petitions, and would
only allow the original £200 * for Arabella's
maintenance, judging perhaps that, since the old
countess managed to build so many large and
beautiful houses, she might contrive to support
her grandchild herself. It is certain, indeed, that
no pains were spared with Arabella's education.
She had masters to teach her modern and clas-
sical tongues ; her physical well-being was looked
to ; she lived chiefly in the country, and grew
up, like all the ladies of that date, to be an
active horsewoman, taking part in the constant
hunting parties, and also a good dancer, according to her uncle Charles (p. 62). Her figure in
her portraits is tall and graceful.

In those days most young ladies of rank
received a thorough education, as in Henry
VIII.'s time, when, says Strype,† the king saw
that not only his son, but his daughters were

---

* This pension seems to have been very irregularly paid. See
Gilbert Talbot's complaints to the lord treasurer, Lansd. MSS.,
art. 39, p. 58.

† "Eccles. Mem.," vol. i. p. 402.

well educated " in good learning, and in the
knowledge of the learned tongues as well as in
other accomplishments. Which example of the
king many noble men following, bred up their
daughters under the best learned men, whom
they fetched from the universities. And many
young women now arrived to very considerable
attainments in the tongues and philosophy."
Under Elizabeth, also, encouraged by the royal
example, the education of women of rank
reached a high standard, and Arabella, with the
great future her relatives believed to be before
her, received every possible advantage.

In her childhood, indeed, Arabella was in a
fair way to be spoilt, ruling like a queen over
her stern old grandmother and her aunts (see
p. 72); and at this time, and for several years,
it is certain that Bess and her sons, the Cavendishes—probably also her step-son, Gilbert
Talbot—built many ambitious hopes upon the
child's claims to the succession. It was not till
she saw no further chance of a crown upon the
head of one so near to her, that the inevitable
rebellion of the high-spirited girl against the

countess's strict government made Bess turn from her once-beloved "juell." As yet these hopes had not proved futile, and in 1583 Leicester, the queen's favourite, showed that he considered the child likely to be a person of importance by a secret project which he and the countess concocted together of an alliance between Arabella and Leicester's infant son (by Lettice Knollys), the Baron of Denbigh.

The first to mention this plan outside the family is Lord Paget, who says in a letter * to the Earl of Northumberland, on March 4, 1583, "A friend in office is very desirous that the queen should have light given her of the practice between Leicester and the countess for Arabella, for it comes on very lustily, insomuch as the said earl hath sent down the picture of his baby."

Mary Queen of Scots, who had ample opportunity of hearing the Shrewsbury family's affairs discussed, and showed a constant interest in her "little niece," also mentions this matrimonial scheme in a letter to Mauvissière (March 21, 1583). She begs him to tell Elizabeth privately

* State Papers, Eliz., Dom., 1581-1590, vol. clix. p. 8, MS.

that nothing had alienated the countess more from her than "the vain hope which she has conceived of setting the crown of England on the head of her little girl Arbella, and this by means of marrying her to a son of the Earl of Leicester." Such a scheme seems of little real importance when one considers that Arabella was only eight, and her betrothed six years younger; but such was the forced precocity of childhood in those days, that Mary reports the children were told of their engagement, and that they exchanged portraits! Great caution was used by both parties lest Elizabeth should hear of the plan, but, no doubt through the letter quoted above, the news came round to her ears only too rapidly. Her anger was aroused as usual by a matrimonial project undertaken without her advice and sanction, and the favourite fell under a temporary cloud at court. Before a year had passed, however, the threatened storm was finally averted by the premature death of the poor little *fiancé* (July, 1584), aged three years. Leicester raised a tomb in Warwick Church over the body of the " noble imp," with an inscription relating that he was a boy of great hope and promise. It seemed as if a blight had fallen from heaven on the innocent offspring of Leicester's union with the widow of the elder Earl of Essex—the mother of Leicester's successor in the queen's favour, the younger earl.

The queen herself first started the idea of a marriage between Arabella and her cousin James, in 1584, which, except for the disparity of age and character, would have been, from a worldly point of view, a most appropriate match ; but in spite of every inducement being used to press the Scotch king to consent, he would not give any direct answer, though he was angry with Leicester * when he heard of his project to marry his son to Arabella.

Walsingham † wrote to Wotton a year later, again suggesting that James should wed Arabella or, failing her, the daughter of the King of Denmark ; but the young king was at this time too fond of his liberty to marry, and four years

* Calendar of State Papers, Scotland, Sept. 6, 1584, p. 486.
† Ibid., 1585, vol. xxxvii. p. 47, MS.

after, though he had meantime definitely refused
both ladies, he suddenly sailed off to Denmark,
and brought back Princess Anne, one of those
suggested before, as his queen.

It was in 1584 also that the project, to which
we shall refer later, was first bruited by the
King of Spain, of a marriage between the
Duke of Parma's son and the little heiress.

Of the child herself we now for the first
time get a glimpse from one outside her family.
While the project for her marriage to Leicester's son was under discussion, in the summer
of 1583, Sir Walter Mildmay, Chancellor of the
Exchequer, had paid a visit to Sheffield, to see
after the affairs of the state prisoner. He wrote*
from there to Walsingham, and incidentally
mentioned Arabella, who seems to have made
an impression on him by her attractions both
of mind and person. He speaks of the "little
lady" as "a very proper child, and to my
thinking will be like her grandmother, my old
Lady Lenox." He encloses a letter (not now

* Calendar of State Papers, Scottish Series, Mary Queen of
Scots, vol. xii. p. 83, MS.

in existence) which he has persuaded the child
to write to the queen, and Arabella sends it with
a pretty message that " her humble duty and
daily prayer is for her Majesty."

Family dissensions were then, as usual, raging
fiercely in the Shrewsbury family. The earl and
countess had long been at open war, the earl
vainly beseeching the queen to allow him to
divorce his wife ; but Elizabeth steadfastly refused to permit the scandal. On one occasion
she even sent for the troublesome pair, and made
them sit on stools, one on each side of her, while
she delivered a moral lecture, and forced them to
make up their quarrel. Bess was by no means
an easy woman to live with. Her soul revelled
in intrigues for the advancement of her favourite
children, while she behaved most unjustly, not
only to her step-children, but also to some of
her own offspring. Both the Cavendishes and
Talbots were now connected by marriage,
Gilbert Talbot's wife being Mary Cavendish,
Bess's daughter ; while the countess's eldest
son, Henry Cavendish, had married the earl's
youngest daughter, and took the part of his

step-father and father-in-law against his mother. At this time Gilbert Talbot, influenced by his wife, was on the old countess's side, and Arabella was often given over to the charge of her uncle and aunt, going with them up to London as she grew older. In May, 1584,* a quarrel about her staying with the Talbots ensued between the earl and countess, and the estrangement of Lord Talbot and his father was thereby increased. The earl, having ordered that Arabella was to be removed from the Talbots' care, *commanded* his wife to receive the child, which she at first refused to do, not only because she wished her to stay on with her daughter Talbot at that time—which was just when her scheme for the betrothal with little Lord Denbigh had been discovered by the queen—but also because her husband used the word "command" in his message. Leicester interposed on the countess's behalf, and this quarrel was apparently patched up.

In July, however, another and more serious

* Unpublished Talbot Papers ; Spencer MSS. ; State Papers, Eliz., Dom., vol. xiii. p. 29 ; Beale to Walsingham, MS.

difference ensued over some landed property
which the earl had presented to his wife on
their marriage for her sons, the Cavendishes,
and now, since William and Charles Cavendish
always took their mother's part against him, he
bitterly repented his gift. It was on this occasion that the earl sued in vain for the queen's
permission for a legal separation from his unruly
wife, and received instead a command to take
her back again and to behave well and cour-
teously to her. Such was the miserable atmosphere in which the child Arabella spent her
early years, and there is, indeed, no wonder that,
as she grew older, she should have moved
heaven and earth for release from her grandmother's care.

When she was twelve years old (1587)
Arabella was first presented at court, and that
she was well qualified to appear there we learn
from a letter* written by her uncle, Charles
Cavendish, in which he tells us, "It is wonderful
how she profiteth in her book, and believe she
will dance with exceeding good grace, and can

* Hist. MSS. Commission Report, iii. p. 42.

2587.] *FIRST APPEARANCE AT COURT.*   63

behave herself with great proportion to every
one in their degree." In the same letter he
says that "my Lady Arbell hath been once at
court. Her Majesty spake unto her, but not
long, and examined her nothing touching her
book." It seems to have been Elizabeth's
habit to put her young court ladies through a
kind of *viva voce* examination on their first
presentation to her. Old Lord Burghley, her
friend almost from her birth, had taken a great
fancy to the intelligent child, whose title to the
earldom of Lenox he had acknowledged, and
tried in vain to secure for her.

Now, we read in her uncle's letter, she had
the honour of supping with the great lord-
treasurer, after her presentation to her Majesty.
"She dined in the presence, but my lord-
treasurer bade her to supper; and at dinner, I
dining with her, and sitting over against him,
he asked me whether I came with my niece or
no? I said I came with her. Then he spake
openly, and directed his speech to Sir Walter
Rawley, greatly in her commendation, as that
she had the French, the Italian, played of

instruments, danced, wrought [needlework], and writ very fair; wished she were fifteen years old; and with that rounded Mr. Rawley in the ear, who answered him it would be a happy thing. At supper he made exceeding much of her; so did he [in] the afternoon in his great chamber publicly, and of Mall, and Bess, [and] George, and since he hath asked when she shall come again to court."

The Queen of Scots had been executed (February, 1587) shortly before Arabella's first appearance at the court, and Elizabeth seems to have made much of the child as a kind of foil to James's pretensions. She was treated, therefore, with great consideration, taking precedence of the nobles, and even dining with the queen—a mark of high favour—till, naturally enough, people began to look upon her as the successor to the throne. One day Elizabeth herself pointed out Arabella to the wife of De Chateauneuf, the French ambassador, saying, " Look at her well; she will one day be even as I am (*toute faite comme moi*), and will be a great lady (*une maîtresse dame*). But I shall have gone before her (*j'aurai été devant elle*). She is a girl," she added, "of much talent, and speaks Latin, Italian, and French very well." Whether Elizabeth had serious intentions of naming the child as her heiress is extremely doubtful, but for a time she found it convenient to allow people to think so, and to make her a foil to James's pretensions, her English birth giving her some advantage over her cousin's claims. In August of this year the French ambassador, after describing Arabella as having "much understanding," speaking "Latin, French, and Italian well, sufficiently handsome in the face," adds she would without doubt "be the lawful inheritress of the crown if James of Scotland were excluded as a foreigner."

By January of the next year Arabella had returned for a while to her country solitude, and writes * on February 8 from Fines, one of the old countess's numerous country houses, the earliest letter extant in her own handwriting.

* Report of Hist. MSS. Commission, iii. p. 420. The original in the possession of Mr. John Webster, Q.C., of Edge Hill, Aberdeen, "written," it is said by Mr. Inderwick, in his interesting memoir, "in a small and distinct print-like hand of the Italian school, different to her large writing later on."

" Good lady grandmother," she says, " I have sent your ladyship the endes of my heare, which were cut the sixt day of the moone on Saturday last, and with them a pott of gelly which my servant made. I pray God you finde it good. My aunte Cavendisshe was here on Monday last; she certified me of your ladyship's good health and dispositione, which I pray God longe to continue. I am in good health. My cousin Mary hath had three little fittes of an agew, but now she is well and merry. This with my humble duty unto your ladyship, and humble thankes for the letter you sent me laste, and craveing your dayly blessinge I humbly cease. Your ladyship's humble and obedient childe,

" ARBELLA STEWART." *

Arabella went up to town and to court again some time this summer, and that old Lord Burghley continued to take notice of her is shown by a French postscript which she adds to

---

* Arabella spelt her surname *Stewart* or *Steward* at this time, but in her later letters it is nearly always *Stuart*.

the letter in which her uncle and aunt, Gilbert and Mary Talbot, with whom she was staying, take leave of the lord-treasurer, before going back to the country. The letter is dated from "Our pore lodginge in Collman Strete, this xiii. July, 1588," and we give Arabella's French exactly as it stands in the manuscript.* "Je prieray Dieu Mon^{sr.} vous donner en parfaicte et entiere santè, tout heureux, et bon succès, et seray tousjours preste à vous faire tout honneur et service.—ARBELLA STEWARD."

In November Arabella was at Wynfield (Winfield), an estate in Derbyshire belonging to the Shrewsbury family, in the care of Nicholas Kynnersley, probably a trusted steward, or perhaps one of the girl's numerous tutors. He writes † the following report to the old countess: "My Lady Arbella, at eight of the clock this night, was merry, and eats her meat well, but she went not to the school these six days, therefore I would be glad of your

---

* Lansd. MSS., 34, p. 145. Also printed in Ellis's "Letters," 2nd series, vol. iii. pp. 66, 67.
† Hunter's "Hallamshire," p. 118.

ladyship's coming, if there were no other reason."

That in the next year (1589) the child was still in favour with Elizabeth is shown by a letter* of her uncle Gilbert's from the court (July 1), in which he says, "The queen asked me very carefully, the last day I saw her, for my Lady Arbella." A proof of the affection with which he regarded his niece is shown by the end of the same letter. He first ends with, "Our prayers to God to prosper my Lady Arbella," and adds in the postscript, "God bless her with all His blessings." Early in this year (April 26, 1589), however, the queen finally gave up† her inquisition of Arabella's title to the Lenox lands, though she doubted that the Shrewsburys would be willing to do the same, since they had offered to prove her title by the laws of the realm. However, henceforth we hear no more of the Scotch inheritance.

But the disputes over Arabella's English estates were not yet over. In 1589 there was a lawsuit about the manor of Smallwood (see

* Hunter's "Hallamshire," p. 119.   † Murdin, p. 635.

p. 216), in Cheshire, on her behalf, and Thomas
Fowler, executor to Margaret of Lenox, was
written to by Lord Burghley's commands for
evidence to help in defending the said lands,
which seem to have formed part of the
Lenox English estates and Lady Margaret's
lands.   No result or further mention of the suit
appears at that time; but as late as September,
1604,* we find one Egerton the defendant in a
case against Arabella about the same estate,
and James I. writing to the Earl of Derby,
Chamberlain of Cheshire, to ask him to be
present at the court of assizes, and, with the
advice of the justices, to take care that Arabella's cause be not injured.   The letter is
subscribed by Popham † the chief justice, with
his opinion that the command is reasonable.
Whether Arabella finally obtained her estate
we do not know, but it is probable that it had
passed into her possession in 1589, and that the
said Egerton was her tenant.

Arabella had now reached the age (fourteen)

* Calendar of State Papers, James I., Dom., 1603–10, p. 153.
† The first owner of Litlecot House.

appointed for her to receive the Countess of
Lenox's legacy, which had been meantime
left in the charge of Thomas Fowler, who had
long gone to live in Scotland. Unfortunately
for Arabella, he had not obeyed the Queen of·
Scots, who had ordered him by a warrant,*
dated from Sheffield, September 19, 1579, to
deliver them up to the Countess of Shrewsbury,
to be kept in her hands till Arabella was the
right age to receive them, or, should she die
before, to give them to James. Fowler, however,
carried the casket with him to Scotland, and
Bothwell, in a border raid, seized upon all the
unfortunate man's goods and chattels, including
the jewels. Thomas seems to have died just
afterwards (early in 1590), and his son William
writes in June, 1590, to complaint to Burghley
of the theft. James meantime seized on the
jewels, and not only ordered the payment of all
sums due to Thomas Fowler to be made to him,
but also detained the valuables in compensation,
so he said, for legacies due to him from his

* State Papers, Scottish Series, Mary Queen of Scots, vol. xi.
p. 18.
† Calendar of State Papers, Scottish Series, pp. 576, 577.

grandmother, but never paid by her executor. For more than a year William Fowler, aided by Burghley's remonstrances on Arabella's behalf, endeavoured to get them back ; but it was of no use, and finally they seem to have been sold by the Scotch king, who was always in want of money. Arabella, however, did not suffer for want of jewels, since we find her wearing beautiful pearls and other valuable ornaments in all her pictures—probably family ones belonging to her mother ; some are even said to have been left to her by her aunt, Mary Queen of Scots.

By the death of the old Earl George (November 10, 1590), the Shrewsbury family, Talbots and Cavendishes, became more split and divided amongst themselves than ever, and the strife grew daily worse. Bess seized the executorship of the estates which had been left to the younger Talbots, in consequence of the heir Gilbert's dissensions with his father, but resigned by them. Furious quarrels over money matters, therefore, ensued between the countess and her old ally, now the new earl and her enemy; he being on bad terms both with his own brothers the Talbots, and with the Cavendishes. Before he died, the poor old earl, whose later life had been embittered by his wife's conduct, and also by the troubles consequent upon the presence of the Queen of Scots in his household, spoke much of his family trials to a confidential servant. Amongst other things he told him * "that he feared the Lady Arrabell would bring much trouble in his house by his wife and her daughter's devices, and therewithall he clapped his hand sundry times upon his breast, saying, 'Here it lies; here it lies. Do you not know one Dr. Browne,' said he, 'a cunning fellow? He is a great man with my daughter Talbot and the Cavendishes. . . . That same Browne is a masker in this house, and my wife and her daughter have great affairs with him, and are dealing with some of the heralds about matters which must be kept from me (for at this time I am a great block in their way). I know Gilbert Talbot will be too much ruled by those—for they do with him what

* State Papers, Eliz., Dom., vol. ccxxxiii. p. 73, MS.

they list, and so I have told his friends, but
all will not help. . . . I know that the queen
affecteth not Gilbert Talbot, both for those
matters he took part with my wife in against
me, and for this Lady Arrabell. She was wont
to have the upper hand of my wife and her
daughter Talbot, but now it is otherwise (as it
is told me), for that they have been advised by
some of their friends at the court that it was
misliked.'" The queen seems to have objected
to her young relative being treated as a person
of consideration, and bowed down to by her
relations, and before long, indeed, she was to
be most despotically used by her grandmother,
who thus laid up future troubles between herself
and her high-spirited granddaughter.

CHAPTER IV.

JESUIT PLOTS AND MARRIAGE PROJECTS.

1590–1602.

ARABELLA'S favour at court was now rapidly on the wane, chiefly because of the matrimonial schemes and suspicious plots which were seething round the innocent girl. As early as 1586 * the English Catholics were conspiring to gain possession of her person, in order to marry her to a foreign prince, and she was barely fifteen (1590) when their schemes, supported by the Pope's influence, took a definite shape. The elder son of the famous Alexander Farnese, Duke of Parma, was the candidate proposed, the third in the long series of suitors destined to sue in vain for Arabella's hand. The chief difficulty in the way, however, was that the first

* Calendar of State Papers, Scottish Series, Mary Queen of Scots, 1586, p. 1012. Cipher Letter, September.

bridegroom proposed (the elder son) married while the negotiations were proceeding ; and the second son was a cardinal, and therefore under vows of celibacy, but the Pope readily undertook to release him from his obligations, in order to make the marriage feasible. In him, the direct descendant of Edward III. through the marriage of John of Gaunt's eldest legitimate daughter with John I. of Portugal, the Romanists saw a new claimant for the English crown, whose rights, if coupled with Arabella's, would, they thought, prove irresistible to the nation.

But these very pretensions made it impossible to propose the match to Elizabeth, and underhand means were therefore devised to bring it about without her knowledge. The Pope sent spies to England to attempt to gain possession of the young heiress's person, Sir William Stanley, one of the most active of his agents between Spain and England, being the chief of those employed. In the confession of James Young,* a Jesuit (taken in August, 1592), one

* Strype, "Annals," vol. iv. p. 142.

of the numerous plots is unfolded. A conversation is reported between Stanley and Dr. Stillington, another Catholic, which took place in Spain some time in 1591. Stanley promised Stillington that he should shortly be employed in the service of a lady of whom they had often talked, "If we had her, the most of our fears were past for any one that could hinder us in England. It is Arbella, who keepeth with the Earl of Shrewsbury, whom most certainly they will proclaim queen, if their mistress should now happen to die. . . . But here is Symple," saith he, "and Rowlston, who, like cunning fellows, have promised to convey her by stealth out of England into Flanders ; which, if it be done, I promise unto you she shall shortly visit Spain, and, as I judge, they will prove men of their word."

Stanley afterwards spoke at a supper-party of Arabella, without naming her, only calling her "an unmarried young lady," as "the greatest fear they (the Scotch party) had, lest she should be proclaimed queen" on Elizabeth's death. One of his listeners, a priest called Christopher, from whose confession * we extract the information, was so impressed by this remark that he afterwards asked Robert Tempest, a Catholic exile in Paris, what it meant. "He answered that very shortly he trusted to God to meet with her here at Bruxells, for that one Symple, a Scot, and one Rowlston, had undertaken to convey her out of England. The lady doth abide with an earl, whose name I do not remember. And she is allied to the Queen of Scots."

The young lady's portrait was to be obtained † for the Duke of Parma to see, Hilliard, the miniature-painter, to be the artist ; and as there are two miniatures now in existence, taken at this time by Hilliard, it is probable that one of these is the portrait which was sent abroad, perhaps brought back by one of the numerous agents when the Parma match fell through.

Throughout the year 1592 the Pope's agents were exceedingly busy over the " Parma " marriage, as it was called, and it seems that

* Strype, "Annals," vol. iv. p. 148, April, 1592.
† Calendar of State Papers, Eliz., Dom., 1591-94, pp. 99, 209, MS.

Arabella's secretary, one Morley—afterwards dismissed on suspicion by the old countess (p. 84)—was extremely active in the business ; * also Moody, a servant of Sir Edward Stafford's, was employed beyond the seas to negotiate the match. Mary Talbot, Gilbert's wife, herself a Roman Catholic, was suspected of trying to convert her niece. " The queen," we are told,† " daily bears more and more a bad conceit of the Earl of Shrewsbury and his countess for the sake of the Lady Arbella, which has been evident in a late quarrel between his lordship and the Stanhopes." ‡ Later on Mary was accused of having had Mass said in the girl's presence.§ In fact, the wildest rumours were rife as to Arabella's matrimonial prospects.

* Calendar of State Papers, Eliz., Dom., 1591-94, pp. 117, 209, 244, MS.

† Ibid., p. 342.

‡ Mr. Inderwick (" Side-Lights on the Stuarts," p. 37) says that Sir John Stanhope's stirrup-leathers were cut by some of the Cavendishes, the Talbots taking Stanhope's part, and that the two parties libelled each other, and brought on themselves several Orders of the Privy Council. See Sloane MSS., 4161, pp. 7–12.

§ 1598. See Inderwick, ibid., p. 35, from unpublished Talbot MSS.

About 1590, a plan seems to have been set
on foot abroad for a match between her and
the young Earl of Northumberland (Henry
Percy, the ninth earl, died 1632), which is
mentioned in the State Papers.*   De Thou †
actually affirms that the two were privately
married ; but there is no shadow of evidence
for this astonishing assertion, nor trace of any
connection between Arabella and the earl in
the family papers, and the affair was apparently
only one of the numerous abortive schemes
started on the other side of the Channel.
Whether the reports were true or false mattered
little to the queen ; it was enough for her to
know that conjecture was rife as to the future
of her young relative, since, whether by marriage
or by birthright, that future involved the succession to her crown.   Hence it can be easily
understood that Elizabeth came to look upon
the girl as her personal enemy, or rather as a
tool in the hands of her enemies, and gradually
withdrew from her every mark of favour, till,

* Calendar of State Papers, Eliz., Dom., 1581–90, p. 708, MS.
† "Romance of the Peerage," vol. ii. p. 364.

as the years went on, Arabella was practically banished from the court, and compelled to live almost as a state prisoner in Derbyshire. But as the queen withdrew the light of her countenance, James seems to have wished to show some favour to his cousin, and in December, 1591, he wrote her an affectionate letter.* "Although the natural bonds of blood, my dear cousin," he says, " be sufficient for the good entertainments of amity, yet will I not abstain, having now so long kept silence till the fame and report of so good parts in you have interpelled me. And as I cannot but in heart rejoice, so can I not forbear to signify to you hereby what contentment I have received hearing of your so virtuous behaviour, wherein I pray you most heartily to continue, not that I doubt thereof, being certified of so full course of nature and nourriture, but that you may be the more encouraged to proceed in your virtuous demeanour, reaping the fruit of so honest estimation, the increase of your honour, and joy of your kindly affected friends, specially

* State Papers, Scottish Series, Eliz., vol. xlvii. p. 123, MS.

of me, whom it pleaseth most to see so virtuous
and honourable scions arise of that race whereof
we have both our descent." He ends by promising to "frequently visit" his cousin with
his letters, and asking her to let him know
from time to time of her estate by her own
hand ; but although, from some of Arabella's
allusions later on, she evidently carried on a
correspondence with the Scotch king, the only
one remaining is that above given, while none
from Arabella to him are extant.

James was evidently interesting himself on
his cousin's behalf, for in 1592 he renewed the
project of a marriage between her and Esmé
Stuart, Duke of Lenox—who, says a letter to
Burghley, "longeth after Arbella"—by which
Arabella's father's titles and Scotch estates
would be restored to her ; the king also
proposing to make Lenox his successor.
But Elizabeth, suspecting a confederacy with
Spain and the Catholics in the background of
this seemingly disinterested offer, sternly refused her consent, "uttering very harsh words
and of much contempt against the King of

Scotland." * The next suitor he proposed was
the Earl of Arran, who, as early as 1585,† had
been said to " hold intelligence" with the little
girl Arbella.

The innocent cause of these ambitious
schemes was so closely guarded by her redoubtable grandmother that the Pope's emis-
saries found it impossible to carry her off.
Bess watched over her charge like a dragon,
and, in reply to a letter of warning from
Burghley, received September 20, 1592, after
the discovery of the conspiracy above mentioned, writes ‡ on the 21st, from Hardwick,
a full account of all the precautions she had
taken to ensure her grandchild's safety.

" My good lord," she says, " I was at the first
much troubled to think that so wicked and
mischievous practices should be devised to
entrap my poor Arbell and me, but I put my
trust in the Almighty, and will use such dili-
gent care as I doubt not but to prevent what-

* Winwood, p. 4.
† Calendar of State Papers, Eliz., Dom., 1585, p. 255, MS.
‡ Lansd. MSS., 71, fol. 2, from original; printed in Ellis's
" Letters," 2nd series, vol. iii. p. 165.

soever shall be attempted by any wicked persons against the poor child. . . . I will not have any unknown or suspected person to my house. . . . I have little resort to me ; my house is furnished with sufficient company. Arbell walks not late ; at such time as she shall take the air, it shall be near the house, and well attended on. She goeth not to anybody's house at all ; I see her almost every hour in the day ; she lyeth in my bedchamber. If I can be more precise than I have been, I will be. I am bound in nature to be careful for Arbell ; I find her loving and dutiful to me, yet her own good and safety is not dearer to me, nor more by me regarded, then to accomplish her Majesty's pleasure, and that which I think may be for her service. I would rather wish many deaths then to see this or any suchlike wicked attempt to prevail." She then describes how a seminary-priest, one Harrison, had stayed with his brother only a mile from Hardwick Hall, on two several occasions, the first time about a year before, and now hearing that he was again there, she had sent her son

William Cavendish to apprehend him, but he had already escaped from the neighbourhood. As a further proof of her vigilance, she tells how she had parted with Morley (see p. 78), who had been her reader for three years and a half, merely because he seemed discontented at not getting an annuity that had been promised him ; and, although not a Papist, she did not consider him to have enough forwardness in his religion. She has now supplied his place, and adds that she will only have those about the place "that shall be sufficient in learning, honest, and well disposed, so near as I can." She winds up by saying that William Cavendish had written the letter at her dictation, as her head was bad, but neither Arabella "nor nobody else" knew of it. Arabella's relations seem to have acted with great circumspection at this critical period of her history, but the poor girl's life must have been far from happy, living under her grandmother's stern and vigilant rule, and guarded like a state prisoner.

Meanwhile the plots grew thicker. A newsletter,* dated 1593, states that Spain makes no account of Arabella, because she is not a Catholic; though in July, 1594, Thomas North † writes from Munich to the Earl of Essex about an interview he has had with the Spanish legate touching the " beauteous and virtuous " Lady Arabella. " They seem to study," he says, " how some plot may be laid for her being conveyed out of England." In this year (1594) appeared the Jesuit Father Parsons's famous book on the English succession. The King of Spain was nourishing a wild dream of seating himself and his children on the English throne on Elizabeth's death, by right of his double descent ‡ from John of Gaunt ; and Father Parsons's book, written under Spanish influence, was designed to prove his claims. In this pamphlet, which was spread all over the Continent and smuggled into Eng-

* Cecil Papers, Hatfield, No. 541.
† Ibid., vol. xxv. fol. 65.
‡ The daughter of John of Gaunt, by his second wife, Constance of Castile, married Henry III., King of Castile, and was Philip's paternal ancestress ; while by his mother, the eldest daughter of the King of Portugal, he was also descended from John of Gaunt's first wife.

land, the claims of the various candidates were fully set forth, and attention was thus drawn, more persistently than ever, to Arabella's place in the succession. The Jesuits disposed of her, as of all the other English or Scotch claimants, by excluding their royal ancestors or progenitors as "disinherited, tainted with treason, or bastards, or heretics," * and declared the only true heirs to be the King of Spain and his issue. The Pope, however, affirmed the rights of the elder branch of the house of Portugal, the Farnese; his favourite plan being that Rainutio,† Alexander's elder son, now Duke of Parma, should succeed by his birthright to the English crown, but, should the nation object to a foreigner, he fell back upon the idea of uniting Arabella's claims with the house of Parma, by marrying her to Rainutio's brother, the cardinal.‡ Parma him-

* See "Lettres du Cardinal d'Ossat," edit. 1714, vol v. pp. 46-49, au Roi, Nov. 26, 1601.

† Rainutio's house had a prior claim to Philip, in that they represented the *male* branch of the house of Portugal, his being the *female*.

‡ "Lettres du Cardinal d'Ossat," edit. 1714, vol. v. pp. 46-49, au Roi, Nov. 26, 1601.

self, it was said, in 1598,* did not care for
Arabella, she being by a second marriage, and
entangled with difficulties.   There had, in fact,
in 1595,† been a rumour that she was to be
proved illegitimate, through her great-grandmother Margaret of Scotland's left-handed
marriage with Angus, her great-grandfather.

A letter ‡ from a prisoner in the Tower to
Sir E. Coke (June, 1595), gives a good idea
of the state of feeling about Arabella on the
Continent at this time.   " I understand," he
says, "that forasmuch as the Duke of Brignola
and the Prince of Parma entitled § themselves
also by Edmund Crookback, as also to Portugal, that one of them with consent of the other
should offer unto her Majesty to marry with
the Lady Arbella, and to become enemy to
Spain ; but this seems to have been a device
in the old Prince of Parma's days [Alexander],
for now Fitz-Herbert and Owen affirm the

* Calendar of State Papers, Eliz., Dom., 1599, p. 212, MS. ¡
† Ibid., 1595, p. 29.
‡ Cecil Papers, vol. xxiii. fols. 85, 86.
§ John of Gaunt's first wife, the mother of Philippa, Queen
of John I. of Portugal, was Blanche, granddaughter of Edmund
Crouchback, Henry III.'s second son.

Lady Arbella's father bastard. But it was
thought that if Sir Thomas Wilkes had come
as he was expected, that Charles Paget had
revived this motion again, hoping that, in
regard to a common peace, to have quietly
enjoyed Portugal and the Low Countries, the
King of Spain would have consented thereto,
and this was said to have been Cardinal
Allen's devise for the present tolerating of
Catholics in England. Others said that if
Sir Thomas Wilkes had come there had been
an offer made of the King of Spain's own son
for the Lady Arbella." The writer then goes
on to speak of the King of Scots' fears about
the succession—how afraid he was lest the
queen should advance Arabella by some act
in her lifetime ; but that, on the other hand,
this was not probable, since Arabella's friends by
her mother's side, the chief of whom (Gilbert,
Earl of Shrewsbury) was of so irregular and
imperious a nature, were at enmity with
Elizabeth's favourite counsellors, who would
certainly be displaced if they came to power.
James was, indeed, now working himself up

into an agony of fear lest his claims to the succession should be set aside for those of his English-born cousin.   In 1596 a rumour * was afloat that Elizabeth intended to keep James in subjection, and was already treating with Henry IV. of France to repudiate his childless wife — which Henry had long had thoughts of doing—and marry Arabella, promising to make him her heir.

Henry's own view of the proposed match was by no means an impassioned one, as we see by Sully's report † of it.   "I should have no objection," he said to the minister, "to the Infanta of Spain, provided that with her I could marry the Low Countries; neither would I refuse the Princess Arbella of England, if, since as it is publicly said the crown of England really belongs to her, she were only declared presumptive heiress of it.   But there is no reason to expect that either of these things will happen."

In spite of the French king's open indiffer-

---

* Calendar of State Papers, Scottish Series, 1590, p. 716.
† Miss Cooper's "Life of Arabella Stuart," vol. i. p. 127.

ence to the plan, James seems to have implicitly believed in its possibility, perhaps because he had learnt by experience how impossible it was to calculate on Elizabeth's next move. In any case, he took a most imprudent and unpatriotic step, actually writing to Philip II., with an offer to become a Papist, and make a league with Spain against their common enemy, the Queen of England. The Spanish king, however, repulsed his advances, and at last James, who had married Anne of Denmark in 1589, consented to take the advice of his wife's relations, and await Elizabeth's death before stirring further in the matter.

Another of the reports * of the day affirmed that Arabella was shortly to be conveyed to Spain, "that she was inclined to it, and that her common speech was that she thought no match in England good enough for her;" the writer, Captain North, adding that "he had commission from her to treat with foreign princes." But credit must be sparingly given to these rumours, and there is no evidence that

* Birch Memoirs, vol. ii. p. 307 : Letter of Captain North.

Arabella knew of, much less took part in, the many plots for her abduction. She herself remained in the background, under the care of her grandmother, while her future was discussed in every court in Europe. Scarcely a year passed that her name was not coupled with a fresh suitor. In the winter of 1599 the report * of a proposed match between her and Duke Matthias was sent to Cecil (who had, on Lord Burghley's death in 1598, succeeded his father as Elizabeth's most trusted counsellor). Another and even vaguer rumour † seems to have selected the young Earl of Gowrie, afterwards notorious in the Gowrie Plot, who was a visitor to the English court in 1600, as another suitor; and it was further asserted that the queen was in favour of the project. The only direct news of Arabella herself is a letter ‡ from Lady Dorothy Stafford,§ one of the court ladies, to the young Countess of

* Calendar of State Papers, Scottish Series, 1599, p. 779.
† "Romance of the Peerage," vol. ii. p. 365.
‡ Hunter's "Hallamshire," p. 120.
§ Lady D. Stafford was buried in St. Margaret's Church, Westminster.

Shrewsbury, thanking her and her niece, in the queen's name, for their New Year's gifts, which her Majesty had accepted very graciously, taking "an especial liking to that of my Lady Arbella," which was a lawn scarf or head-veil, "cut-worke florished with silver and silk of sundry colours." *   The countess seems to have been writing to the queen on her niece's behalf; for Lady Dorothy continues, "It pleased her Majesty to tell me that whereas, in certain former letters of your ladyship's, your desire was that her Majesty would have that respect of my Lady Arbella that she might be carefully bestowed to her Majesty's good liking; that, according to the contents of those letters, her Majesty told me that she would be careful of her, and withal hath returned a token to my Lady Arbella, which is not so good as I could wish it, nor so good as her ladyship deserveth in respect of the rareness of that which she sent unto her Majesty. But I beseech you, good madam, seeing it pleased her Majesty to say so much unto me

* Nicholls's "Progresses," vol. iii. p. 451.

touching her care of my Lady Arbella, that
your ladyship will vouchsafe me so much
favour as to keep it to yourself, not making
any other acquainted with it, but rather repose
the trust in me for to take my opportunity
for the putting her Majesty in mind thereof,
which I will do as carefully as I can."

In 1601 came the sad fate of the brilliant
favourite, the Earl of Essex, which, since he had
always shown great kindness to Arabella, was,
she tells us herself, a great shock to her. It is
from this time also that the old queen began
to fail, and for the next two years little else
was talked of but the great question of the
succession, while intrigues, in which the Shrewsbury family no doubt took part, centred round the
two probable successors—James and Arabella.

It was about this time that the Scotch king
worked himself up again into a great state of
agitation over a false report which reached him,
that his cousin had been at last induced to
change her religion. The following letter * to
Sir Henry Howard expresses his feelings on

* Miss Cooper, " Life of Arabella Stuart," vol. i. p. 159.

the subject : "I am from my heart sorry," he
says, "for this accident fallen to Arbell, but as
nature enforceth me to love her as the creature
nearest of kin to me next my own children, so
would I, for her own weal, that such order were
taken as she might be preserved from evil
company, and that evil-inclined persons might
not have access unto her to supplant, abusing
of the frailty of her youth and sex ; for if it be
true, as I am credibly informed, that she is
lately moved by the persuasion of the Jesuits
to change her religion and declare herself a
Catholic, it may easily be judged that she hath
been very evil attended on by them that should
have had greater care of her when persons so
odious, not only to all good Englishmen, but to
all the rest of the world, Spain only excepted,
should have access to have conferred with her
at such leisure as to have disputed and moved
her in matters of religion." Though there was
certainly no truth in the story of her perversion,
it was perhaps with good reason that James
agitated himself, for the chief thing which had
made his cousin unwelcome to foreign powers,

and to the powerful Catholic party at home, was her religion. No doubt also that her aunt, Lady Shrewsbury, "a most dangerous woman, and full of her father's inventions," would have liked to shake her niece's Protestant faith, and in spite of the dragonish old dowager, must have had many opportunities of secret conversation. But Arabella was now a woman of twenty-six, and no weak and feeble creature, as James seems to think, bowing with every breeze, but one not easy to move in any direction, as we shall see presently. The Jesuits, in fact, gave her up in despair, and an anonymous writer declares in April, 1602, that "the Jesuits say that Lady Arbella is a notable Puritan, and they hold the Turk more worthy of a place than she."

At this time some news of our heroine may be found in Father Anthony Rivers's secret correspondence * with the famous Father Parsons, who was in hiding on the Continent, England having been too hot to hold him since his book on the succession. On March 27 (1602) Rivers

* "Foley Records," vol. i. pp. 24, 26, etc.

writes, " The arrival of the Duke of Nevers is daily expected . . . the general opinion is that he cometh of curiosity to see the court and country, but in special I hear he desireth secretly a sight of the Lady Arbella ; for that some great person here, bearing the French in hand that it shall be in his power to dispose of the succession after her Majesty's death, by preferring whom he please to match with the said lady, this duke, albeit a married man, being a great favourite, is fed in hope thereof for himself (if his wife die) or some friend, and thereupon, under colour of some other embassy, undertaketh this voyage. How probable this may be I leave to your consideration, only this much I can assure you, that a house is here preparing privately in London, where the good lady, with those with whom she liveth, are expected after Easter." He gives us in the same letter a strange and tragic account of the great queen's failing powers. " The ache of the queen's arm is fallen into her side, but she is still, thanks to God, frolicky and merry, only her face sheweth some decay, which to conceal, when she cometh in public, she putteth many fine cloths into her mouth to bear out her cheeks, and sometimes as she is walking she will put off her petticoat, as seeming too hot when others shake with cold." On March 30 Arabella is " shortly to come to town ; " but the problematic suitor never put in his appearance, as he went off to the archduke's instead of visiting England. By the summer Rivers reports that the ache in the queen's side is increasing, and the like beginning also in her thigh ; however in July she " hunted . . . with good show of vigour and ability," but her feebleness is again shown when, in September, she "refused help to enter her barge, whereby, stumbling, she bruised her shins."

CHAPTER V.

A MYSTERIOUS EPISODE.

1602–1603.

WE have now reached a most mysterious episode in Arabella's career—an episode which gave rise to much speculation at the time, and has received an appearance of truth from subsequent events. At the time, the rumour, which coupled her name with that of the boy William Seymour (grandson of the Earl of Hertford), was with justice regarded as a ridiculous and lying report ; but since in 1610 she actually contracted a marriage with the same youth, the truth of the gossip of 1602 has seemed proved for later historians. To her contemporaries, however, who were unable to look into the future, the idea of a match between Arabella and a schoolboy was considered a preposterous one, as we shall see, for though the general talk connected her with an unknown suitor, William's name was the last to obtain credence.

On July 26, 1602, the first warning of the approaching storm is given by the same Jesuit, Father Rivers, from whose letters we have quoted before. He reports, " I hear some have an intention to marry the Earl of Hertford's second son with Arbella, and to carry it [the succession] that way, but these *supra nos nihil ad nos.*" Again, later on, the rumour connecting the lady and the Seymour family persistently gained ground; now it was with Lord Beauchamp himself (the Earl of Hertford's elder son), whose wife had lately died, that she contemplated matrimony; now with *his* eldest son, Edward, a boy of sixteen; and, as we have seen, even the name of the second brother, William, who was only fourteen, was mentioned as her *fiancé.* As the direct descendants of Katharine Grey, Lord Beauchamp and his sons were dangerously near the throne, and, when the gossip about Arabella's connection with the Seymour family reached Elizabeth's ears, in January, 1603, the old queen was

roused to a state of wrath and agitation piti-
able to witness. By some papers, including
several letters from Arabella herself, amongst
the Hatfield MSS.—all (except a few passages
from one letter given in Edwardes's "Life of
Raleigh") hitherto unpublished—the mystery
which surrounds this period of her life is by
no means cleared up, but it is possible to discern
a motive in the lady's mind for raising this
tempest in a teacup.

We learn by the dying confession of one
Starkey,* whose suicide (about February 1,
1603) gave rise to fresh speculations, that Arabella had been for some time past most unhappy at home. Starkey had got into trouble
by sympathizing with her griefs, and had offered
to help her by delivering letters or messages for
her when he got to town. The poor man complains of "the servitude and homage wherein
I have lived more than ten years, having taught
one of Mr. William Cavendish's sons six or
seven years without any consideration for my
gains, and being then enjoined to teach another

* See Part II. B, No. 1, vol. ii. pp. 92–97.

his A B C ; and besides my living, which was
given me, being indirectly detained from me by
Mr. Cavendish" for seven or eight years.   Tired
of this hard life, Starkey left Hardwick some
time in the summer of 1602.   At Easter (1602),
he says, Arabella had told him "that she thought
of all the means she could to get from home,
by reason she was hardly used (as she said) in
despiteful and disgraceful words, being bold,
and her most plagued withal, which she could
not endure, and this seemed not feigned, for
oftentimes, being at her book, she would break
forth into tears."   After he had gone to town,
he and Arabella exchanged various communi-
cations, which he declared were only connected
with books, and she sent him a silver escutcheon
for a New Year's gift.   Rumour, however, had
already connected his name with hers, partly,
it appears, because he had had his own initials,
J. A. S., which were interpreted by scandal-
mongers as John (his Christian name) and
Arabella Stuart, engraved on a Bible.   Arabella
certainly tried hard to get Starkey to help her
to escape from her grandmother's yoke, promis-

ing, if he would, to make him her chaplain when she moved ; but he declares that he "supported her rather to endure her grief and discontent patiently, than by an inconvenient course to prejudice herself." For his own part, he was busied, he says, about the recovery of his parsonage, and when all efforts failed, he hanged himself.

He was probably put under custody on suspicion of having aided and abetted the culprit Arabella, for he says, "Now they have taken from me, first liberty, then my living, my life, and my good, I trust you will be satisfied."

There is no doubt that Arabella had made a confidant of Starkey. He tells how she had not only complained to him that her grandmother had threatened to take away her jewels, which she had prevented by sending them away into Yorkshire, but much greater matters which "I forbear to set down," and that he had done various commissions for her, which amounted to over £300, only £219 having been paid up to the time of his death.

Arabella certainly had some dealings with the Seymours in the winter of 1602, before the report of her engagement was spread abroad, but from Starkey's confession, her own protestations, and the testimony of her servants, it seems tolerably clear that her one object was to escape on some pretext or other from her old grandmother's iron rule, and the secret mission to the Earl of Hertford undoubtedly had this, and this alone, for its motive, the marriage project being merely a blind.

John Dodderidge, her messenger, afterwards confessed * all that he knew of the affair. About three weeks before Christmas, 1602, he says that Arabella first asked him if he would go a little way for her, and not long afterwards told him she wanted him to go an errand of a hundred miles. The man, who was in old Lady Shrewsbury's service, naturally replied he dared not for fear of his mistress's displeasure, and that the errand would certainly lose him his situation. The young lady, however, declared

* See Letters of John Dodderidge, Cecil Papers, Hatfield, vol. cxxxv. fols. 108–110.

that he need not care, as he would "find friends,"
meaning her uncles Henry and William Cavendish, who were deeply involved in her plans,
and herself. Dodderidge, therefore, consented
to go, and was then told he must make his
way to Amesbury, and see one Kirton, the
Earl of Hertford's lawyer. The substance of
his message to Kirton was to the effect that,
some time before that year, the Earl of Hertford had commissioned his lawyer to speak
to a Mr. Owen Tydder, in Wales, an old
servant of Lady Shrewsbury's, "to move my
Lady of Shrewsbury [the dowager] about the
marriage betwixt his lordship's grandchild,
the Lord Beauchamp's *elder* son, and the Lady
Arbella."

This fact, if true, is of the utmost importance,
as proving that the idea originated with the
Seymour family, though it was no doubt taken
up by Arabella as a good way of thwarting and
escaping from her grandmother; it also proves
that there was then no idea of a marriage
between her and William, her future husband,
but that his elder brother, Edward, was the

one proposed for her. Lady Shrewsbury had refused to listen to the project, as she would not seem to deal in it without the queen's knowledge, and there, as she thought, the matter ended. Arabella now, however, took advantage of the earl's former idea, and wished Dodderidge to tell his lawyer that, if his master were "desirous of the same still, he must take some other course."

At this point the message broke off, for Dodderidge's scruples caused him again to hesitate about going on so dangerous a mission, and Arabella made an abortive attempt to get Starkey to do it for her. Starkey, however, refused, and Dodderidge at last agreed to go. The place and person to which he was bound were now altered, and he was ordered to go straight to the old Earl of Hertford in London, and to deliver the same message, but in slightly different and fuller terms. After reminding the earl of his proposal, Dodderidge was to say that "the matter hath been thoroughly considered by some of her [Arabella's] friends ; for they think

your lordship did not take an ordinary course
in your proceedings, for it was thought fitter
that my Lady Arbella should have been first
moved in the matter, and that the parties might
have had sight the one of the other, to see how
they would like [each other]. For that if his
lordship were desirous of this still, he might
send his grandchild, guarded with whom his
lordship thought fit, and he could come and go
easily at his own pleasure either to tarry or
depart." The ostensible purpose of their visit .
was to be to sell land or borrow money ; if they
came they must bring some token with them to
show who they were, since evidently Arabella
did not know the boy even by sight.

In a note of instructions * written in her own
hand and given to Dodderidge, there is a most
interesting passage showing that she had an
intimate acquaintance with the details of the
family history. She suggests that the boy
should come disguised as the son or nephew of
one of his attendants, an "ancient man," and
bring, as proofs of his identity, "some picture

* Part II. B, No. 2, vol. ii. p. 98.

or handwriting of the Lady Jane Grey, *whose hand I know ;* and she sent her sister a book at her death, which were the very best they could bring, or of the Lady Katharine, or Queen Jane Seymour, or any of that family which I know they, and none but they, have."

Dodderidge was told he might name Arabella's uncles, Henry and William Cavendish, as approving of his mission, though he said he never had had conference with them personally on the subject. But Henry's part in the plan is proved conclusively by the fact that, though he only returned to Hardwick the day before Dodderidge went, on Christmas Eve, he not only knew that the messenger started next day, but his niece borrowed a horse for the man from him. On Christmas Day, " presently after dinner, [he] went out at the gates, and, calling me to him, told me his man should deliver me a horse, which he did at the place where his horses stood, some little distance from Hardwick House."*

* Letters of John Dodderidge, Cecil Papers, Hatfield, vol. cxxxv. fols. 109, 110.

Dodderidge was destined to meet with a different reception to what his lady expected. He arrived at Tottenham on Monday, December 30, about three in the afternoon, and demanded a private interview with the earl, refusing to tell his business to any one else. After some parley he was admitted to the dining-chamber, and, falling on his knees before the earl, delivered his message out of earshot of the household, who stood apart looking on. Hertford became so impatient that he refused to let the man proceed, and the servant who gives the account * from which we quote, entered the room just then, and found his lordship "looking very much moved and disturbed." Hertford declared that the marriage was contrary to his wishes, though he certainly did not deny Dodderidge's imputation that he had "sent into Wales . . . to deal with one Owen Tydder [Tudor] to persuade the countess to consent." However, he scolded the unfortunate messenger for having had the presumption to come to him

* Cecil Papers, Hatfield, vol. cxxxv. fol. 179 : the Report of the Earl of Hertford's man.

on such an errand, and then shut him up in a
private room till he could "conveniently send
him to the Privy Council," and told him to set
down his business in writing, which he did afterwards in letters dated January 2 (see above).
Dodderidge's *alias* seems to have been "Good,"
and the servant calls him by that name in his
report.

About nine the same evening the earl
examined him again, but he could learn nothing
further, nor could his servants, although they
went and discoursed with him, and the writer
of the report slept in his room, with the key
under his pillow. The poor wretch naturally
enough was in a great state of mind, did not
sleep a wink that night, and during his detention
wrote a letter to his lady, which is pathetic
in its anxiety and distress. He tells her his
entertainment was contrary to his expectation,
and that the earl will not believe, unless she
satisfies the bearer of the note, but that he
was concerned in some plot, and she in danger.
He beseeches her, therefore, to take pity on
his estate, though he would be sorry to do

anything that might be offensive to her in any way.

Although Dodderidge knew no more than he had already told the earl, yet Hertford insisted on carrying him off to Cecil on the evening of the 31st, in spite of his tears and protestations. It was, therefore, about January 1 that the business came to the queen's ears, and Sir Henry Brounker was immediately sent to Hardwick, where he arrived on Friday, January 3, to investigate the matter.'

Brounker's task was an exceedingly difficult one. He had to deal with two determined women—one justly offended by what she considered the unwarrantable deception which her granddaughter had practised on her ; the other equally angry, and boiling with the repressed indignation of months of restraint and severity.

Arabella's own letters during the next three months can only be compared to those she wrote years after, when once more a marriage project—no longer a shadowy one—roused her sovereign's anger against her. Her agitation is often so great that her tears drop on the paper, and her hand trembles so that she can scarcely hold the pen, while her words are frequently the mere outcome of irritation and mortification, and cannot be taken as containing any real meaning. As we proceed to examine these letters in detail, we shall discover also a tone of pique, as if she would fain have had a love affair ; though the mysterious suitor, of whom we never hear again after this period, is doubtless a blind, and only referred to in order to agitate the queen and her counsellors. It is admissible, however, to wonder whether the poor lonely woman had really conceived a fancy for some unknown person, possibly for the deceased Earl of Essex (see later), since it seems scarcely possible that she, whose affections were so ardent and passionate in after-days, could have lived heart-whole till nearly the age of twenty-seven. The letters themselves are printed in Part II. (for the first time) *in extenso.* We now intend to follow, as well as the information before us allows, the course of events at Hardwick during the three months of 1603 which preceded the old queen's death.

When Brounker* arrived at Hardwick, he found the old countess walking up and down the long gallery—which may still be seen by visitors to that interesting old house—with her unruly granddaughter, and her own dear son William. Before Arabella the wily queen's messenger contented himself with delivering a gracious greeting from Elizabeth to the countess, but soon drawing the old lady away to the further side of the gallery, he gave her the royal letter. After she had read it, her countenance changed, and Sir Henry, seeing her fear, consoled her by the assurance of the queen's continued favour, and asked for a private interview with Arabella herself. This took place in the same gallery, out of earshot of the countess and her son. Brounker began by giving a message of thanks from the queen for a New Year's gift, and tried to soften the scolding that was coming by adding that Elizabeth had lately observed her young cousin's behaviour to be more dutiful than it was wont to be. He then proceeded to

* See his letters to the queen: Cecil Papers, Hatfield, vol. cxxxv. fols. 113, 115, 118.

break the queen's displeasure and its cause to her, warning the wilful young woman that the whole affair had been so openly confessed that there was no denying it, unless she would have the queen believe that, in her ardour, she had laid aside her duty and affection, "whereas otherwise, upon the naked laying open of the fault both of herself and others, she should show her desire to explain any error committed by her."

During the delivery of this exhortation the culprit stood silent before him, only showing her agitation by the coming and going of her colour. Arabella's first impulse was to deny everything, even to saying that, though she knew John Dodderidge well, and had seen him a little before Christmas, she thought he was now with his friends. Brounker, who had the man's confession of January 2 and his letters in his possession, admonished her for being so obstinate and wilful; but, finding he made little impression, he produced the papers. Telling her it was no use denying her share, as everything was discovered, he asked her who had been the prime mover of the marriage project. She would only tell him what he already knew— about Owen Tydder, and the Earl of Hertford's lawyer, though she admitted having had a project of sending Dodderidge to the earl, but had revoked her instructions. At last, in despair, Brounker left her, and told her, as she would not do it in words, to confess her faults in writing.

The letter which she handed him the next morning was no better, being " confused, obscure, and in truth ridiculous ; " and he told her it was not fit for the queen to receive. Whereupon she wrote another, little better than before, "which made me believe," Sir Henry sagely remarks, that " her wits were throughout distracted either with fear of her grandmother or conceits of her own self." Neither of these letters is extant. Finally, seeing the documents were conclusive, she was obliged to confess to their truth, though he could get nothing further out of her, except a prayer for the queen's pardon. She also declared Hertford to have been acquainted with the matter from the beginning; but Brounker would not believe this, judging her to have been deceived about it, and the earl guiltless.

About January 10 Brounker left Hardwick for London, not arriving at Lambeth, owing to an accident on his way, till the morning of the 13th, and as he was suffering from a swollen face, and the queen was also unable to receive him at once, he writes, describing his visit, to the queen and Council (January 15 and 16). Meantime, on the 12th he had written, ordering one Sir Richard Bulkeley to examine (January 15) the offender Owen Tydder.* Little information was, however, elicited from Tydder, except a confirmation of the fact that the idea of such a marriage had been broached, but he thought it had been some three or four years before. This would, of course, have been impossible, since the elder boy, Edward Seymour, was now only in his seventeenth year, and it is very likely that Tydder found it more convenient to forget the right date. Some confusion seems, however, to have arisen between another man

* Cecil Papers, Hatfield, vol. cxxxv. fols. 120, 122.

called Owen and himself, for Tydder denied all
acquaintance with Kirton, Hertford's lawyer,
but said that one Owen had spoken to him on
the subject of the Seymour match, and had
asked him to get him speech with Arabella :
this he had refused. Tydder himself had served
the old countess for twenty years, and when he
had left her service in the summer of the year
before (1601), his eldest son had become page
to Lady Arabella. We shall find the youth's
name mentioned in her letters later on.

CHAPTER VI.

THE PLOT THICKENS.

1603.

WHILE these investigations were slowly proceeding, Arabella and her grandmother remained at Hardwick, at daggers drawn with
one another. The old countess had sent a short
note * (January 9) before Brounker left, thanking
the queen for her gracious message, and pro-
testing her ignorance of Arabella's doings. So
offended, indeed, was she because her charge had
not confided in her, that she begs the queen to
place her elsewhere till she learns " to be more
considerate, and after that it may please your
Majesty either to accept of her service about
your Majesty's most royal person, or to bestow
her in marriage." As a bribe to Brounker to
further her desires, which here coincided with

---

* Cecil Papers, Hatfield, vol. cxxxv. fol. 112.

Arabella's own, she pressed at parting a purse of gold into his hand.

In this her great trouble and perplexity, Arabella herself thought of her friendly aunt Mary; and on the 15th she wrote * to one Hacker, a man in the young Countess of Shrewsbury's household, urgently requesting her aunt to come at once to her, "with the like speed she would do if my lady my grandmother were in extremity . . . for the matter I would impart to her, and will neither for love nor fear impart to any other till I have talked with her, it imports us all, and specially her and me, more than the death of any one of us ; and yet she hath no cause to doubt, much less to fear, that any harm how little soever should happen to any of us so she come in time, that I be not constrained to take the counsel and help of others who would make their own special advantage without that respect of any but themselves that I know she would have. It is not for fear of a chiding, but some other reason, . . . that I beseech her not to take

* Cecil Papers, Hatfield, vol. cxxxv. fol. 123.

notice of my sending for her, and she shall be
bound by promise to keep my counsel no
longer than it please her after she know it ; for
else it is such as I dare and mean to trust a
mere stranger withal, and will win her Majesty's
good opinion of whoever is employed in it."

At the same time, Bridget Sherland, who had
probably been one of Arabella's waiting-women,
writes,* telling Hacker that her lady is re-
strained of her liberty, and that he had better
come and see her (Mrs. Sherland) at Sutton, as
well as sending for the young countess to go to
Hardwick. Hacker replied that he was afraid
to venture to either place—Sutton being close
to Hardwick ; nor did Mary Talbot respond to
her niece's appeal. A few days later a certain
Bradshaw, whose wife is doubtless the same
Mrs. Bradshaw who was afterwards Arabella's
faithful waiting-woman and friend, consented
to carry a letter from Arabella to Brounker.
This letter has not been preserved, but a short
note,† craving pardon from the queen for her

* Cecil Papers, Hatfield, vol. cxxxv. fol. 124.
† Part II. B, No. 3, vol. ii. p. 99.

offence, and asking her Majesty to signify through the old countess, "whose discomfort I shall be till then," the forgiveness she hoped and expected, may be placed at this time.

For about a fortnight no answer was vouchsafed from the court, and matters became more and more strained, till on the 29th Lady Shrewsbury writes * again about "this unadvised young woman" to the queen. The poor countess is evidently in a great state of perplexity and anxiety, since her grandchild kept her in constant agitation by mysterious speeches and hints that she could be taken out of her hands if she wished ; and Bess shrewdly suspects that "another match is in working." So irritated, indeed, is the once doting grandmother, that she declares she would not "care how meanly soever she [Arabella] were bestowed, so as it were not offensive to your Highness." In reply to this came a most sensible letter † from Cecil and Stanhope, who seem to have acted for the queen throughout

* Cecil Papers, Hatfield, vol. cxxxv. fol. 127.
† Ibid., fol. 128.

the affair. The young woman, they tell her grandmother, is "to avoid idle talks and rumours, whereof there is aptness in most men to take liberty in this time." Some base companions, in the queen's opinion, have taken advantage of Arabella's youth and sex to deceive her with the idea that Hertford wished her to marry one of his grandsons, which, from the incongruity of ages, is, on the face of it, untrue. Vexed as her Majesty is with Arabella's concealment of the matter, she is willing to pass over the offence this time, on condition that she takes this mishap for a warning, and confides any other project to her grandmother or the queen. Lady Shrewsbury is not to exclude people or to guard her house any longer (which causes gossip), but everything is to return to its accustomed routine; a trustworthy gentlewoman is to keep her eye on Arabella's doings, but otherwise no extraordinary restraint is to be used, and she may ride and walk about as usual. The queen, however, will not hear of relieving the countess of her troublesome charge, and the two ladies were therefore obliged to remain under the same roof for the present.

An undated letter * from Arabella to her sovereign may be placed at this period, since it contains her thanks for the queen's clemency. It is the first and the calmest of a series of most extraordinary documents, all written by the young lady herself, evidently in great distress and confusion of mind.   The language is, as usual in letters addressed to the great queen, and especially by those who had offended, fulsome in its flattery; and Arabella considers it politic to attribute her chief unhappiness to her banishment from the royal presence.   The only natural and unaffected passages are those in which she complains of her old grandmother, without whose knowledge she confesses she has done many things, but all of them "such as (if she had not been stricter than any child, how good, discreet, and dutiful soever, would willingly obey) she should have had more reason to wink at than to punish so severely as she hath done."   About the same time she penned an enormously long letter

* Part II. B, No. 4, vol. ii. p. 100.

to the old lady herself, which Bess hastened to enclose with one * written the same day (February 2) from herself to the queen's ministers.

Lady Shrewsbury was both perplexed and puzzled by Arabella's conduct. In vain did she sermonise her charge, and entreat her to confess her faults to her; all she obtained was a lengthy written discourse, full of mysterious hints and allusions to a secret lover, which baffled even the shrewd Bess's penetration. This unnamed lover is an excellent stalking-horse, which Arabella maliciously uses to agitate and perplex the queen and her advisers, the "two grave and honourable councillors," as she somewhat satirically dubs Cecil and Stanhope. For three years, she asserts,† have she and "her dearest and best-trusted, whatsoever he be," beat their brains over some undiscoverable project—probably merely how the lady could escape from her grand-mother's guardianship, to which marriage would have appeared the only solution. She and her friend deliberately planned and executed "that

* Cecil Papers, Hatfield, vol. cxxxv. fol. 129.
† See Part II. B, No. 5, vol. ii. pp. 103-113.

which we knew for a short time would be offensive to her Majesty, your ladyship, the Earl of
Hertford, and divers others, and work an effect
which I am most assured will be most accep-
table to her Majesty, and it is even the best
service that ever lady did her sovereign and
mistress." She also promises she will reveal
some secrets of love concerning herself to the
queen, if allowed to have the space of one month
to clear herself, and liberty to send to any
Privy Councillor; but to the queen only will
she be accountable, and not to the countess.
She is obviously misleading the old lady, however, when she avers herself in a position to dis-
close matters which will offend none but her
uncle and aunt of Shrewsbury and Charles
Cavendish, and will make herself as merry at
their expense as they did last Lent by playing
a practical joke upon her. As a matter of fact,
Arabella was probably secretly on terms of
friendship with the relations she pretends to
abuse,* and before many months she and the
young Shrewsburys were more intimate than

---

* See also her examination, Part II., vol. ii. p. 124.

ever. For several pages the letter continues in much the same strain about her mysterious lover, promising to make the queen merry over the whole affair, but reiterating her resolve only to unravel the mystery to the queen in person.

It was just at this critical time that Starkey committed suicide, which, the French ambassador reports (February 2),* aroused many suspicions, especially when the poor wretch's extraordinary confession, referred to earlier (p. 100), of his dealings with Arabella, was discovered. No blame certainly was given to her for her connection with the tutor; but there is little doubt that she had once hoped to use him as a means to the end, perpetually before her eyes, of escape from the countess. Throughout the country rumour rapidly † succeeded rumour. James had somehow won the reputation of a hot temper and a "sanguinary humour," and for some time it had been remarked (De Beaumont tells the French king) that people at court had spoken more freely of Arabella's virtues than before, and had of late excused her with much fervour to

* King's MSS., vol. cxxii. fols. 740–748.   † Ibid.

the queen. Reports were rife, too, of a letter which Hertford was said to have written to her about a match with his youthful grandson ; but the lady herself declared to Brounker that this was only an invention to laugh at the old earl, while gossip either leaned to this view or suspected that Arabella's impatience to be married had led her to desire an alliance more fit for her rank and quality than any other in England.

Four days after the strange epistle to her grandmother, Arabella wrote * to Cecil and Stanhope, to express her anger that, in spite of the queen's pardon, her grandmother continued to treat her with great strictness, quite beyond the terms of the royal instructions. She now asks that definite answers may be given to her questions whether she may have free choice of her servants, and send for and talk in private to any friends she likes; whether she may have "the company of some young lady or gentleman for my recreation, and scholars? Music, hunting, hawking, variety of any lawful disport, I can procure or my friends, as well as the attendance

* Part II. B, No. 6, vol. ii. pp. 113–118.

of grave overseers, for which I think myself most bound to her Majesty, for it is the best way to avoid all jealousies." She begs that the length of the time of her disgrace, and the precise rules by which her obedience is to be tried, may be set down. She shows also much vexation that Lady Shrewsbury had sent "the firstfruits of her scribbled follies" to court, and requests that Sir Henry Brounker may be again sent down to see whether the affair will prove as foolish as they seem to suppose from her trifling manner of handling it. Again is the mysterious "beloved" referred to, with a promise to confess all, if she may receive "two lines from the queen's own hand;" but, had she only known it, Elizabeth was already far too failing to have written to her kinswoman, even had she consented to do so.

At twenty-seven, as Arabella herself remarks, it was certainly hard to be treated as an irresponsible child; but in truth the hysterical and extraordinary tone of her letters at this period may well have alarmed her friends for her sanity. That she was, however, in full posses-

sion of her senses when she chose, is shown by
a curious letter * of February 16, to her cousin,
Edward Talbot, of whose part in the business
nothing has hitherto transpired. By this it
appears that Arabella had received a satisfactory
answer to her requests for liberty, and permission to choose her own friends. While she has
been accused of continuing a comedy, Edward,
it seems, is suspected of making a tragedy ; but
both, she declares, may wash their hands in
innocency. She begs him to come to Hardwick, and take a message thence for her to the
court ; but the young man took good care not
to venture into old Bess's clutches, though he
evidently was, like his step-uncle, Henry Cavendish, on Arabella's side, and secretly working
for her.

The worry and discomfort of her position now
took serious effect on Arabella's health. For a
fortnight she was obliged to have a doctor in
close attendance, but till her mind was at rest
it was impossible for her to find any ease. "So
wilfully bent" was she, her grandmother com-

* Part II. B, No. 7, vol. ii. p. 119.

plains * (February 21), that she made a vow
not to eat or drink while she remained under
the old lady's roof, and, her will proving the
stronger of the two, Lady Shrewsbury was
obliged to send her to Oldcotes, about two
miles from Hardwick. So wearied is the old
countess of this perpetual war, that she also
begs for the speedy sending down of Sir Henry
Brounker. Her letter is answered at once by
Sir Henry in person, bearing a written reply †
from the two ministers, in which the countess
is again exhorted to treat the young lady with
proper respect, "lest the world should think she
were to be used as a prisoner."

The queen, though unable any longer to
write, was still able to read letters, and she confesses herself, like every one else, utterly puzzled
by Arabella's mysterious hints. Since it was
impossible to settle the business from a distance, Lady Shrewsbury and her son William
Cavendish are to consider Brounker as the royal
representative and authority.

* Letter to Cecil, Part II. B, No. 8, vol. ii. p. 120.
† Part II. B, No. 9, vol. ii. p. 122.

The messenger's visit turned out, however, but a fool's errand. On March 2 Arabella was examined,* but her answers only threw the good Sir Henry into greater perplexity than ever. To every question about her mysterious lover, she would only give the name of the King of Scots—the one person in the realm about whom no conjecture as to an intrigue with his cousin could be made. For this reason we may well conclude that James was made the butt of her ladyship's humour, and credited with being her confidant. Some of her assertions she had, however, the grace to confess were mere "conceits" of her fancy, and to one or two questions she refused an answer. On the same day Arabella wrote† a declaration, asserting by all she held holy that she was "free from promise, contract, marriage, or intention to marry, and so mean to be whilst I live, and nothing whatsoever shall make me alter my settled determination but the continuance of these disgraces and miseries, and the peril of the King of Scots

* See examination, Part II. B, No. 10, vol. ii. pp. 124-130.
† Part II. B, No. 11, vol. ii. pp. 131-135.

his life;" by which she appears to mean if James were in danger of death, and she chosen as Elizabeth's successor. In exaggerated language she declares death would be more pleasing to her than marriage, if she had her choice of " all Europe, and loved and liked 'them better than I did or shall do any." It is, however, in mockery that she says she has delivered all her reasons to Sir Henry, since her " reasons" are so puzzling that, were it not for our own judgment that her one and only object was to create a scandal, and so escape from her grandmother's keeping, there would seem no sense in her doings. As it is, it is pretty evident that she continued to hold that goal before her, and her grandmother, whom one is now obliged to pity, also again entreats for her speedy removal, for when Brounker arrived she had, of course, to return to Hardwick from Oldcotes. In her despair, Arabella vainly named a day to Sir Henry for her removal, but both he and Lady Shrewsbury besought her not to stand on days and times. "She is so wilfully bent," cries Bess *

* Part II. B, No. 12, vol. ii. pp. 135–137.

(March 3), " and there is so little reason in most
of her doings, that I cannot tell what to make of
it.   A few more weeks as I have suffered of late
will make an end of me.   I beseech the Almighty
... to send ... myself quietness in my old days."

Sir Henry left Hardwick on March 4, but
scarcely had he gone than Arabella sat down
again at her writing, and inscribed a lengthy
epistle * to him, still affirming, though she " will
not *swear,* her mysterious friend to be the
King of Scots."   The tone of this letter is
bitter in the extreme, but there is plenty of
sense in it, in spite of hidden allusions to a
threatened attempt to carry her off, and to her
" little, little love."   She complains of having
been made accountable for " idle words, which
is much, and idle conceits, which is more," and
by this very admission shows how little cause
there was to fear a hidden plot in the background of her dark sayings.   " After my cousin
M.," she says, referring to one of her numerous
relatives, probably to Mary Talbot,† Gilbert's

* Part II. B, No. 13, vol. ii. pp. 137–143.
† Afterwards married to William Herbert, Earl of Pembroke.

daughter, "and I had spent a little breath in evaporating certain court smoke, which, converted into sighs, made some eyes besides ours run a-water, we walked in the great chamber, for fear of wearing the mats in the gallery (reserved for you courtiers), as sullenly as if our hearts had been too great to give one another a good word, and so to dinner. After dinner I went in reverent sort to crave my lady my grandmother's blessing. Which done, her ladyship proved me a true prophet, and you either a deceived or deceiving courtier; for after I had, with the armour of patience, borne of (*sic*) a volley of most bitter and injurious words, at last, wounded to the heart with false epithets, and an unlooked-for word, only defending myself with a negative, . . . I made a retreat to my chamber." She then leaves her point to declare how little she now can believe Sir Henry's promise that her chamber should be her sanctuary, since by what was past in the matter of the Lenox lands, she had learnt what small reliance could be placed even on the word of a prince. Returning to her interview

with Lady Shrewsbury, she tells how, wearied by
standing, she went away at a good sober pace,
not running, to her bedroom, her ears battered
on one side by a storm of threatenings from her
grandmother, on the other by a summons to a
parley with her uncle William. Fearing probably
that the latter might undermine her resolution
not to give the names of those who were on her
side (Edward Talbot and Henry Cavendish
were two of them), she, like "a deaf asp," went
her way "without so much as looking behind me
(for fear of Eurydice's relapse)." Her relatives,
however, followed her to her room, where till
midnight the day before she and Sir Henry had
sat scribbling, he his report of her examination,
she the declaration quoted above, which she
had sent by him to court. After a stormy
conflict, Arabella sat down to write her account
of the affair, even while her grandmother and
uncle stood by railing at her for her disobedience.
After reading what she had written to her angry
relatives, Arabella ran downstairs in search of a
messenger; but so difficult was it to get one of
her grandmother's servants to go her errands,

that she was obliged to mount once more to
the " great chamber," where she and her cousin
had paced up and down a short while before.
Her sudden apparition at the opposite door to
that by which she had lately left the room so
thrilled through a group of, " for my sake, mal-
contents," who stood gossiping—no doubt, of her
affairs—that they fell back in surprise and
excitement. To one alone, a certain Chaworth,
who stood hat in hand, and the lady's glove in
his hat, did Arabella address herself. To him
she confided a short letter * and a message,
with which and the above document, describing
the domestic turmoil, did Chaworth ride after
Sir Henry, arriving shortly after him at Lambeth
Marsh. Brounker, to soothe the wilful young
woman, had apparently promised more than he
meant to perform, and she reproaches him in
both letters for his want of faith, her anger
kindled by finding herself still in her grandmother's guardianship.

Poor Sir Henry continued for some days to
be pursued by letters. Arabella's restless pen

* Part II. B, No. 14, vol. ii. p. 144.

must have been employed in writing all day and every day, and though all these letters contain much that had been written over and over again before, a perusal of them rewards us by more details of her life than have been discovered before.

On Sunday, March 6, she sends a note* in praise and recommendation of some young man, whose services, long before offered to her, have now been accepted. This is no doubt the Mr. Chaworth who rode post after Brounker to Lambeth, with the lady's glove in his hat. On the next day follows a letter † of complaint, with which all book-lovers must sympathize. Arabella, whose " dead counsellors " were her truest friends through life, is forbidden even to have her books fetched from her " quondam study chamber " by Owen, her page. This unnecessary strictness was in no way what the queen had commanded, and there is little wonder that the high-spirited young woman breaks out into indignant complaints. Her language in

* See Part II. B, No. 15, vol. ii. p. 145.
† Ibid., No. 16, p. 146.

this letter of March 7 and some of the others is strikingly like the exaggerated religious phraseology of the Puritan times, and one can well believe her when, exasperated by a certain Mr. Holford, who had driven her from her grandmother's presence with laughter, she cries out, "I was half a Puritan before, and Mr. Holford, who is one whatsoever I be, hath shortened your letter, and will shorten the time more than you all"—by which apparently she means that she is inclined to be somewhat strait-laced on the score of amusements and jests. Certainly a few months later, when she shone at James's gay court, her inclination was always to retire to her books, and to avoid the frivolities in which the other court ladies delighted. In a previous letter to Brounker (No. 13) she had also called herself a Puritan.

CHAPTER VII.

THE LAST DAYS OF ELIZABETH.

1603.

PERHAPS the most interesting of all Arabella's strange epistles at this period is a very long one, written * on Ash Wednesday, March 9, in which she laments her position with redoubled grief and lamentations.   The queen will not afford her the ordinary rights of a subject, she complains, and breaks out into wailing: "They are dead whom I loved; they have forsaken me in whom I trusted; I am dangerous to my guiltless friends."   Her tone to Sir Henry is decidedly kinder; were he a private person, she declares she would entrust her secrets to him; but the thought of the two councillors in the background deters her.   The queen, she feels sure, would be gracious to her,

* Part II. B, No. 17, vol. ii. pp. 147–169.

and Arabella had imagined, when Brounker came for the second time and brought her the royal forgiveness, all would be well. But it was not so. Old Lady Shrewsbury had redoubled her strictness scarcely had Sir Henry gone, when Arabella's "wooden yoke" became (in her own forcible language) of "iron."

The tone of this whole letter is most unguarded, but, fortunately for the lady, Elizabeth was even then far too ill to read it. An important circumstance is learnt for the first time from Arabella's own words. We have referred before to the grief she must have felt in the death of the Earl of Essex, and it is no vain conjecture. She now plainly declares herself to have been the favourite's friend, and dares to exclaim, "Doth her Majesty favour the Lady Katharine's husband [Hertford] more than the Earl of Essex's friend? Are the Stanhopes * and Cecils able to hinder or diminish the good reputation of a Stuart, her Majesty being judge? Have I stained her

* Who, as we have seen (p. 78), were enemies of the Shrewsbury family.

Majesty's blood by unworthy or doubtful marriage ? Have I claimed my land * these eleven years, though I had her Majesty's promise I should have it ? . . . Have I forbore so long to send to the King of Scots to expostulate his unkindness, and declare my mind to him in many matters, and have no more thanks for my labour ? " Little did Arabella guess, so secret was Elizabeth's real condition kept, when she complains of not receiving a letter from the queen direct, but always in "the secretary's hand," that she would never see that writing again, never again meet her royal kinswoman face to face, and that even while she was, as she imagined, pouring out her woes and imploring justice from her sovereign, Elizabeth was drawing near her end.

Lengthy as is this last letter of Arabella's to Brounker, we learn nothing new about her present affairs. She again and again reiterates her determination to reveal nothing except to the queen herself, and exclaims, in real or simulated anger, "I will rather spit my tongue

* The Scotch heritage, see Chapter II.

in my examiner or torturer's face than it shall be said, to the dishonour of her Majesty's abused authority and blood, an extorted truth came out of my lips." Two lines from Elizabeth's own hand, she repeats, would have made her trust the queen with "that infinitely dear adventure," the mysterious love-matter she so continually refers to. In old days the queen had been wont to listen to the opinion of "a noble and unentreated mediator, who now holdeth his peace"—either her old friend Lord Burghley, long dead, or perhaps James; the former is the most likely, when his intervention in Arabella's interest in her early days is remembered. Bitterly does the lady complain that, though grown a woman, she is not allowed to grant lawful favours to princely suitors.

It is the anniversary * of the unfortunate Earl of Essex's execution, and she again returns to her friendship with him, and from her own words we learn the manner in which for many years she had been treated whenever she appeared

* He was executed on February 25, 1601, Ash Wednesday.

at court. "How dare others visit me in my
distress," she cries, "when the Earl of Essex,
then in highest favour, durst scarcely steal a
salutation in the privy chamber, where, howsoever it pleased her Majesty I should be disgraced in the presence at Greenwich, and
discouraged in the lobby at Whitehall, it pleased
her Majesty to give me leave to gaze on her,
and by trial pronounce me an eaglet of her own
kind, worthy even yet . . . to carry her thunder-
bolt, and prostrate myself at her feet (the Earl
of Essex's fatal, ill-sought, unobtained desire)
as any Hebe, whose disgraces may be blush-
ingly concealed but not unseen, or Ganymede,
though he may minister nectar in more accept-
able manner? But whither do my thoughts
transport me now? Let me live like an owl
in the wilderness, since my Pallas [Elizabeth]
will not protect me with her shield." After
this outburst the fate of Starkey returns to her
mind, and, instead of laying the blame of his
end on his being disappointed of a living, as
others had done, she declares that the "innocent, discreet, learned, and godly" man was

driven to despair by the greatness of her enemies, and the hard measure she had received.

After twelve years' experience of Arabella,
Starkey not only had not believed her true
grief, but had suspected her of "a monstrous
fault," of which some one had falsely accused
her. Who can tell whether the first conjecture
was not the truest after all, and that poor
Starkey had indeed fallen in love with the
fascinating young lady, and, finding his cause
hopeless, hanged himself? It is certainly a
significant fact that Arabella herself constantly
harps on this string in these letters. For several
pages Brounker's ears are "battered" by recrimi-
nations, and Arabella's elaborate attempts to
justify her foolish conduct in the whole business ;
for were her mysterious lover a fact, or her desire
to leave Hardwick and return to court her only
aim, she certainly might have spared Sir Henry
these lengthy, hysterical, and incoherent epistles.

Back she returns after a while to the Earl
of Essex, for whom she seems to have had a
considerable affection, and it is even possible
that that gallant's friendship with her may have

roused the queen's jealousy, and been one of the causes of Arabella's prolonged banishment from the court.

It is interesting to get an account of the famous anecdote of the earl's rash intrusion into the royal presence on his return from Ireland, from one who must have heard the story at first hand. He had hitherto " ever returned with honour, and was received home with joy. Till— all ungrateful not to be bound more strictly by a letter of her Majesty's hand than all the bonds and commandments of any or all other mortal creatures—he stole from his charge as if he had longed for the most gracious welcome he received ; and was punished for his unmannerly (but I think in any lover's opinion pardonable) presumption of kissing that breast in his offensively wet riding-clothes, with making those mild kind words of reprehension the last that ever his ear received out of his dear mistress's mouth. Of whose favour (not in respect she was his sovereign, as I protest he ever said to me) how greedy he was even in the Earl of Leicester's time (before he so fully possessed it by many degrees, as after, to her Majesty's eternal honour, he did), I, and I doubt not many more better believed at court, are good witnesses. And how, over-violently hasty (after two years' silent meditation) to recover it he was this fatal day, Ash Wednesday * and the new dropping tears of some, might make you remember, if it were possible you could forget."

Here the learned lady, as often happens, breaks out into Latin, but she soon returns to her own tongue, and by the following statement bears out our conjecture that she may have had a tenderer feeling than mere friendship for the handsome, courted young earl. "Were not I unthankfully forgetful," she asks, "if I should not remember my noble friend, who graced *me*, by her Majesty's commandment disgraced orphan, unfound ward, unproved prisoner, undeserved exile, in his greatest and happy[iest] fortunes, to the adventure of eclipsing part of her Majesty's favours from him, which were so dear, so welcome to him ? Shall not I, I say, now I have lost all I can lose or

* The day of Essex's execution.

almost care to lose, now I am constrained to renew these melancholy thoughts by the smarting feeling of my great loss ; who may well say I never had nor never shall have the like friend, nor the like time to this to need a friend in court, spend thus much or rather thus little time, ink, and labour, without incurring the opinion of writing much to little purpose ? "

This whole day, which is so sad an anniversary, she spends shut up alone in her chamber, sending Sir Henry the "ill-favoured picture" of her grief.

The King of Scots is now the subject of her discourse, whom, though unkind, she still loves, and by the declaration of her love had puzzled Sir Henry, who, she says, cannot understand the practical application of the precept to love one's neighbour as one's self. It is interesting here to note that there had been gossip about Arabella and Essex, and she accuses James of having given ear to "the slanderous and unlikely surmise." Again the young lady breaks off to excuse the length of her letter, which she has the grace to call "peevishly tedious." She urges, in extenuation of her diffuseness, that, being allowed no company to her liking, she finds writing the best pretext to avoid the "tedious conversation" of her relations.

Brounker had treated her with short and courtier-like epistles in answer to her pages of manuscript, and Arabella is much offended, as she wishes him to reply to her as a friend, and not only as a commissioner. Not "an angel from heaven," she says, could make him believe the truth of her words ; for, had he believed her complaints, he would have come back when he heard the strict treatment she had received directly he had turned his back. But he preferred to act only as his commission directed, and would not visit her in "sorrow, sickness, prison, and many ways distressed. . . . Had the Earl of Essex the favour to die unbound because he was a prince, and shall my hands be bound from helping myself in this distress, before I confess some fault . . . which I never committed, and renew my suit to you to convert these unwelcome counsellors' letters to a commission to take my head?" As a friend only will she answer him, "upon such security as friends require and take one of another in matters of this nature."

After breaking out into exaggerated religious expressions, Arabella returns to reproaches, which certainly had some truth and justice in them. "How many vain words are spoken! and who dare speak for me? How many wanton favours are earnestly and importunately begged! and who dare humbly, and even once and no more, remember her Majesty to cast her gracious eye upon me, at least with no less favour than I deserve? How many inquisitive questions are asked of me! and how little inquisitive are my friends and acquaintances what becomes of me! What fair words have I had of courtiers and councillors! and so they are vanished into smoke. Who is he amongst you all who dare be sworn in his conscience I have wrong? and dare tell the Earl of Hertford he hath done it?" The letter concludes in the same high-flown strain, Arabella comparing herself to Esther, and declaring the queen's golden sceptre to have turned into a scourge upon her.

Had not the date of her birth long since been decided as 1575, the uncertainty would now be set at rest by her own testimony; for in two of her letters of this period she declares herself to be twenty-seven. Mr. Holford, the man whom Arabella so often accuses of annoying her, seems to have gone to court, and returned with a minute of further instructions * to the old countess from Cecil and Stanhope, dated March 14. In this it is recommended that Holford, as a man of "good religion" and much interested in the young lady, should have access to her. The strange style of her letters, and their dispersion abroad about the country (of which Bess often complains), is inconvenient in many respects; but for all that, the queen will not consent to her removal from Lady Shrewsbury's care, the old grandmother being, however, cautioned to deal more mildly than hitherto with her charge. The "councillors" express much surprise that, since Arabella's letters are disgraceful to herself and her family, her uncles do not feel more keenly in the matter, and

* Part II. B, No. 18, vol. ii. pp. 170–172.

volunteer their opinions how to remedy it to the queen and Council. Another undated fragment * blames Henry Cavendish, and begs the countess to lose no time in letting him and William understand what is expected of them.

The fact that Bess was going quite the wrong way to work with her headstrong granddaughter, is evidently quite clear to the authorities ; for in this minute it is ordered that she should "so fashion all things as the young lady may not mislike her habitation ; " and William Cavendish, "who is a gentleman that can both please her and advise her in due proportion," is henceforth "to ease his mother of that continual care which we see you take, the same being a great trouble to yourself, and more proper for him, whose company is more agreeable unto her [Arabella]."

But four days before this letter was written events had reached a crisis ; Arabella's uncle, Henry Cavendish, had made an abortive attempt, in concert with a papist gentleman, one Stapleton, to carry her off from Hardwick, and,

* Cecil MSS., vol. cxxxv. fol. 168.

as soon as the news reached the court, Brounker was sent down post-haste again, arriving about March 17. He reports * (March 19) that Arabella "has neither altered her speech nor behaviour . . . but desireth liberty. . . . I persuade her to patience and conformity;" but nothing will satisfy her except "her removal from her grandmother," so bitter is her feeling towards the old lady. As for the countess, she is weary of her charge, and William Cavendish unequal to the burden imposed on him. Brounker concealed the reason why he had come down again from Arabella, and pretended that he had come only to see her wrongs righted. She, however, challenged him to tell her the truth, and finally he was obliged to confess the discovery of her attempted escape.

In the examinations † held on March 19 by the royal envoy, some details of this plot escape. Henry Cavendish and Stapleton collected a band of about forty men, divided into several companies, and dispersed about the

---

* Cecil MSS., Hatfield, vol. cxxxv. fol. 174.
† Ibid., 171–173; see vol. ii. pp. 171–175.

country, they themselves and three or four going to a place called Hucknall, about half a mile from Hardwick (March 10), in the expectation of meeting Arabella, one of the men having a "little pillion behind his horse." Some climbed the steeple, to see if the lady were coming, but she never appeared, being watched too closely to get out alone.

Late that same Thursday night old Lady Shrewsbury had written to court * an account of the affair, and by her letter one sees why Arabella never appeared. About twelve that day the young lady had attempted to walk out of the gates, but was persuaded to give up the idea. Two hours later, the countess's "bad son Henry" and his friend Stapleton, tired of waiting, came and boldly asked to see Arabella. Bess allowed Henry to come in, but refused admittance to Stapleton, whom she says she hated, and therefore had not seen for eight years. After a few words together, Henry and his niece tried to join Stapleton outside, but the old lady refused her consent. A very

* Cecil MSS., Hatfield, vol. cxxxv. fol. 167.

stormy scene must then have ensued. Arabella asked indignantly if she were a prisoner, and, looking through the shut gates, conversed with Stapleton, telling him to go to Mansfield, a town about five miles off, and stay there till he heard from her. A crowd of people had collected outside, and heard all that passed, much to Lady Shrewsbury's annoyance. However, at last Cavendish and Stapleton departed, not before the former had tried to arrange a meeting with his niece for the next day, which his mother forbade. Scarcely had they gone than Arabella got ready to "walk abroad," but, of course, was prevented. Her grandmother, in a great state of anxiety, then despatched her account of the affair to the Council, declaring her granddaughter would certainly escape if not soon removed, and recommending her removal further from the north.

Stapleton escaped to London, but Henry Cavendish was sent for by Brounker, and was ordered to go to court to report himself and his doings. Fortunately, however, for Cavendish's safety, the event so long expected took place a few days after Brounker's journey to Hardwick, and with Elizabeth's death Arabella was soon to recover health and liberty, and to return to her usual frame of mind. Brounker himself advised (the 19th) that, since the queen were so near her end, it would be as well to remove Arabella from Hardwick, for danger might arise on her death, William Cavendish being too weak a man to be relied on to keep his charge safely. This advice must have been followed without delay, for before the queen's death, which took place on March 24, Arabella had been sent to the care of Sir Henry Grey, sixth Earl of Kent (a connection of hers—the earl's wife being the daughter of her uncle, Gilbert Talbot), at Wrest House.*

We have thus far exclusively followed the events that took place day by day at Hardwick, the secret history of that stormy period having never before seen the light. Let us now turn for a moment to the court. It can easily be imagined how the bitter memories connected

---

* About nine miles south of Bedford. Arabella visited Wrest again in her progress of 1609 (p. 230).

with Katharine Grey and the Seymours, her descendants, roused the ire of the failing queen, when she heard of a projected alliance between one of them and her young kinswoman. The air was full of rumour, and the names of James and Arabella were on every lip as possible successors to the crown. It is interesting to hear from independent authorities the popular account of the Hardwick mystery. The French ambassador De Beaumont's despatches in the King's MSS., are full at this time of Arabella and her affairs.

We have already given his reports of Starkey's death (see p. 125). The general impression seems to have been wonder that the matter was made so much of, as it was really of small consequence, "seeing the little credit the houses of both parties have." But it was afterwards conjectured, from the agitation shown by the queen, that there must be something greater behind than was at first supposed. De Beaumont,* sensibly enough, however, considers this anxiety only natural and pardonable at the queen's

* King's MSS., vol. cxxii. fol. 149, Feb. 26.

age. The old countess added to the general
uneasiness by raising the country-side about
Hardwick to protect her and her granddaughter,
and De Beaumont says he had heard that she
had been reprimanded for her over-zeal, and
bidden to confine herself to a strict watch over
Arabella's doings.

The popular report of the events at Hardwick is given by the ambassador in a letter
of March 6,* and is wonderfully accurate.
Arabella is carefully guarded by a gentleman
of the court, Brounker ; her letter to Hertford,
he hears, contained only words of courtesy and
credit for the bearer, and nothing about a
marriage, which latter fact was true enough.
But in reply to Brounker's interrogations, she
had confessed herself as promised in marriage
to some nobleman, whose name she would only
reveal to the queen, and, either by artifice or
naïveté, so conceals her meaning that it is
impossible to discover to whom she refers.

The affair perplexes every one, and even the
wisest refrain from giving judgment ; certain

* King's MSS., vol. cxxii. fol. 760.

circumstances connected with it make some esteem the whole business as unimportant. On the other hand, others represent it as of great consequence, and, amongst other reasons for suspicion, allege the great and growing familiarity between Arabella's uncle Gilbert, Earl of Shrewsbury, and Cecil.   De Beaumont himself inclines to think there is "a snake in the grass," but at the same time disbelieves in the existence of any plot to wed Arabella to an Englishman, which would not help her claims against James.   Were it a foreign alliance, such as the late King of Spain had attempted to bring about (referring to the "Parma match") things would be more serious.

About the same time (March 9), an intercepted letter from Rivers [*] gives us more of the common talk.   "That the Lady Arbella had a guard over her, I advertised in my former," he says.   "Since then some have bruited that she is married to the Earl of Hertford's grandson, which is most false.   In course, they

[*] MS. in State Papers, Dom., Eliz., vol. cclxxxvii. p. 50, and printed in "Foley Records," vol. i. p. 53.

give out that she is mad, and hath written to her Majesty that she is contracted to one near about the queen, and in good favour with her, and offering, if he may be pardoned, to name him. Whereon some deem Mr. Secretary [Cecil] to be the man, others Lord Mountjoy, some forsooth Grivell [F. Greville], some one, some another. And now Brounker is again sent unto her, and as it is thought will bring her to Woodstock, where she shall be kept. What the design may be cannot yet be discovered; only it is observed that the Secretary, the Earl of Shrewsbury, and his lady are grown very inward, and great friends, and many secret meetings are made between them, where, after secret consults, they despatch messengers and packets of letters, and this sometimes twice in a week." "The rumours of Arabella much afflict the queen," he adds in another letter; but, in truth, day by day Elizabeth grew less capable of comprehending anything. She was now (see De Beaumont's letter in the King's MSS., 122, of March 9) in such a state "she neither hears nor understands what is said to her;" her favourite Cecil's voice could alone reach her dim comprehension, though the old Tudor could still be roused to resentment by the mention of a hated name. The death of her old friend, the Countess of Nottingham, and the pardon extorted from her to Tyrone, the Irish rebel, added to the dying queen's troubles.

De Beaumont, on March 13,* incorrectly reports that Arabella is already taken from the old countess's care, and a rumour is going about that she is to be declared Elizabeth's successor. But Cecil's secret messengers were all this time flying to and fro from James, and no effort was spared to make the Scotch king's succession a matter of certainty; for this reason, no doubt, Cecil determined to make sure that Arabella was in safe keeping, and so removed her from Hardwick a day or two before the queen's death.

On the 17th Northumberland writes † to James that Elizabeth had now been very unwell for a month. At first it was publicly supposed to be only indisposition of mind, caused by the

---

* King's MSS., vol. cxxii. fol. 766.
† Cecil MSS., Hatfield, vol. cxxxiv. fol. 99.

worry over Arabella and Tyrone and the death
of her old friend, but now it could no longer
be concealed from the country that she was
seriously ill in body. "She sleeps little, will
take no physic, is very weak, and is dull and
lethargic."

Perhaps the most striking account of the
great queen's last days is that given by Ranke.*
How she sat day and night on the cushions "in
deep silence, her finger on her mouth. She
rejected physic with disdain. Most said and
believed she did not care to recover or live any
longer—that she wished to die."

At the very end, when her Council, assembled
(March 23) round her bed, spoke of her successor, her old spirit fired up. At the mention
of Lord Beauchamp's name, she cried, "I will
have no rascal's son on my seat," and, though
she was unable to articulate in words, by signs
clearly indicated James as her successor. At
midnight she, who had raised the prestige of
England above the other countries of Europe,
passed gently away, and, whatever her faults as

* Ranke, vol. i. p. 354.

a woman, to the last she sustained her character as a great and honoured queen.

With her death the rumours and vain gossip about the court were stayed as if by magic. Contrary to the general expectation, no one uttered a word against the peaceful succession of James. The Earl of Hertford came forward to sign the proclamation of the nobles acknowledging the new king, in his own name and that of his son, as representing the younger branch of the royal family, the house of Suffolk. Arabella seemed transformed into another woman, calm and reasonable, which fact alone shows that her strange behaviour at Hardwick must have been acting, in the hope she had always entertained of escape from her tyrant-grandmother. She made a declaration to the effect that she desired no other position than the king allowed her, and remained quietly at Wrest House till he arrived in London.

The queen's funeral was fixed for April 28, and (writes * Dudley Carleton) " the Lady Arbella is to be chief mourner." This, how-

* "Court and Times of James I.," vol. i. p. 8.

ever, was not the case.   It is true that Arabella,
being the late queen's nearest relation, "was
specially requested to have honoured the funeral
with her presence;" but she had the strength
of mind to refuse.   In her spirited reply * we
see how deeply she must have felt her royal
kinswoman's systematic neglect of her of late
years.   "Sith her access to the queen (in her
lifetime) might not be permitted, she would
not after her death be brought upon the stage
for a public spectacle."   The sun of Arabella's
fortunes, clouded for so long, was now, however,
about to shine forth in all its splendour, though
the blackness of perpetual night was destined
all too soon to obscure its brightness.

* MS. Life of Elizabeth, Sloane MSS., 718.

CHAPTER VIII.

1603.

JAMES arrived at Whitehall on May 7, 1603, in high good humour. Not only was he delighted by his peaceful proclamation, so different to the phantoms his fears had conjured up, but his vanity was tickled by the loyal reception he had met with on his progress from Scotland. Mr. Secretary Cecil proved himself this time a true friend to Arabella, for he took advantage of the royal sunshine to press her claims to be set at liberty, and treated with the respect due to her rank, upon the new sovereign.

Arabella was allowed to come up to town to greet the new king, and had a personal interview with him. In spite of her protestations that she would "do all things here-

after that might give his Majesty satisfaction,"
James was much inclined to send her back
to Wrest House ; but Cecil, who had had good
reason to know the difficulties of dealing with
so high-spirited and obstinate a young woman,
counselled another course. He told the king
that "he thought she would not agree to go
thither, nor to any other place as commanded
therunto, for so she might think that she were
still under a kind of restraint ; and that, now
she had spoken with his Majesty, if she had
not given him satisfaction, she might conceive
that she should never be able to give him
satisfaction, and so it would redouble her
grief and affliction of mind, wherewith she had
been too, too long already tormented, and besought him to deal more tenderly with her,
and . . . to send her word . . . that he would
leave her to the charge of her own good dis-
cretion, assuring himself that she would do
nothing of moment whatever without his
privity and good allowance." For his part
Cecil undertook that, while Arabella would
imagine herself free to select her residence, he

and her uncle and aunt of Shrewsbury would so arrange matters that she should "*choose* to be with the Lady Northampton at Sheen." *

To Sheen, therefore, Arabella went at the end of May or the beginning of June, and from there she wrote some letters to Cecil on the subject of a pension—the first of the long series of appeals for money with which she was to assail the penurious monarch through his minister. It seems that Cecil had promised to move the king to provide for his cousin's wants by a fixed annual pension, and on June 14† the lady writes to remind him; it is amusing to note the difference in her tone now that she found herself treated according to her rank, and no longer as a troublesome child. All her old acrimony against Cecil is forgotten, and her letters are no longer verbose and at times hysterical, but short, clear, and to the point.

It was not easy to get money out of James,

---

* For all the above extracts, see manuscript letter of Gilbert Talbot, Earl of Shrewsbury, dated May 18, 1603 (Lambeth MSS., 709, fol. 151).

† See, for letters from Sheen, Part II. C, No. 1, (*a*), vol. ii. p. 176.

more especially a promise of an annual sum;
and so Arabella seems to have found, for on
June 22 * she writes again to Cecil, asking for
some money to meet her present wants, if the
pension could not be had, and on June 23 †
she names £2000 as necessary for her immediate expenses. This request was granted,
for two grateful letters (dated June 26 and 30 ‡)
follow, in which she thanks the minister for
procuring and hastening the king's liberality
towards her, and says that she is "greatly
bound" to his lordship for his kindness in the
matter.

While Arabella was writing these letters
from Sheen, the queen was on her way from
the north. An old manuscript life of Elizabeth
of Bohemia, quoted by Miss Strickland, asserts
that Lady Arabella met the queen in Nottinghamshire, and, joining the royal train, proceeded
with it to Windsor. According to the dates of
the letters quoted above, which are in the lady's
own hand, it is impossible that she can have

* Part II. C, No. 1, (*b*), vol. ii. p. 177.
† Ibid., (*c*), vol. ii. p. 178.   ‡ Ibid., (*d*), vol. ii. p. 179.

gone to meet the queen; for according to
Nicholl's "Progresses," Anne of Denmark only
reached Berwick on June 3, and did not pass
through Nottinghamshire till between the 15th
and 23rd, when she arrived at Leicester. As
the letters from Sheen commence on June 14,
and do not end till June 30—the day the queen
reached Windsor—we have certain evidence
that Arabella was at Sheen during the royal
progress. The manuscript authority further
says that she was appointed state governess to
the Princess Elizabeth ; but this is also an
evident error, as the Countess of Kildare was
appointed to that post on June 5, just after the
royal party had crossed the border. The same
authority asserts that on the day of Prince
Henry's installation as a Knight of the Garter,
Arabella and the little princess watched the
ceremony from a recess in one of the windows
in St. George's Hall, Windsor (July 2); but
there is nothing to corroborate or confute this
assertion, which may well have been true. The
queen hated the Earl of Mar so much, that,
since he was to be one of the new knights, she

refused to be present at the installation, but she held a drawing-room afterwards, which Arabella attended in company with her aunt Mary of Shrewsbury. When we read that all the ladies' dresses were "most sumptuous, and exceeding rich and glorious in jewels," we cannot wonder that Arabella's debts were very large by the end of the year, especially as this was before she had any fixed pension. When Princess Elizabeth was sent to the Haringtons' care at Combe Abbey, in October, the untrustworthy manuscript gives a touching account of the child's parting from her brother Henry, then a boy of nine years old, and also from Arabella ; there is no reason, however, to doubt that Arabella's friendship with Henry included his favourite sister, even at this early period.

After a short visit to the Shrewsburys Arabella went with them to the court—which had meanwhile removed to Farnham—where she was to be henceforth, as the king's nearest relative, a person of great consequence. Her uncle Gilbert seems to have been very anxious about his niece's behaviour under these new conditions, and when he and his wife were obliged to go north of the Trent—he having been appointed Lord Justice in Eyre *—he specially commended her affairs to the care of one Sir William Stewart, probably a relative of her own. Although the king had now been six months on the throne, it had been found impossible as yet to get the vexed question of his cousin's pension settled.

In August Arabella writes to her aunt Mary from Basing, asking her to get her uncle to write to Cecil on her behalf, and "to take notice of his and my Lord H. Howard's crossing the king's intention for my allowance of diet. I think that makes others deny me that the king granted, and makes even himself think anything enough, when so wise counsellors think it too much. You know his inclination to be kind to all his kin, and liberal to all he loves, and you know his protestations of extraordinary affection to me. Therefore I am sure it is evil counsel that withholds him so long from doing for me

* The district north of the Trent.

in as liberal sort or more as he hath done for any." *

Stewart, who was making every effort on her behalf, writes to the Earl of Shrewsbury on September 11 (1603) that "his Majesty is wonderful well disposed" about it; and he beseeches the earl and countess "to continue in writing from time to time your wise and loving opinion to my lady, your honour's most tender and dearest niece, who, I doubt not, in time, with wisdom, patience, and good government, shall both be blessed of God and win her process. For although her virtue and knowledge has been envied of some, yet her ladyship has acquired many favourers, and sundry well affected to her honour and good merits by her good behaviour." † A few days afterwards Stewart's prophecy was fulfilled, and Arabella obtained not only a pension, but a further present of £660,‡ and her diet from the king's table. The "diet" was a certain number of

---

* Part II. C, No. 2, (*b*), vol. ii. p. 181.
† Sloane MSS., 4161, fol. 16.
‡ Nicholl's "Progresses of King James," vol. i. p. 426.

dishes allowed to the members of the royal family and other persons of distinction about the court, with which to feed themselves and their numerous households.

Arabella writes to her aunt Mary from Oxford (September 16), "The king hath under his hand granted me the aforesaid mess of meat, and £800 per annum, and my Lord Cecil will despatch it, I trust, with all speed, for so his lordship promiseth." * On September 17 Cecil writes, "How my Lady Arbella is now satisfied I know not, but the king hath granted £800 yearly for her maintenance, and of it £200 beforehand, and she shall also have dishes of meat for her house." Yet that this pension was not enough for all the lady's needs we see by the constant requests for money later on, and also her numerous debts. There is no doubt that she was extravagant, but at the same time, it must be remembered that, as a court lady, and a near relation to royalty, she was expected to dress very smartly, and appear in a new and gorgeous gown for every festivity, besides pay-

* Part II. C; No. 2, (c), vol. ii. p. 182.

ing the salaries of her numerous household, and keeping up a certain amount of state, all out of a not very large income, though £800, it is true, went further in those days, and a year later it was increased to £1000.* James had also occasional fits of generosity, and would present his cousin unexpectedly with a sum of money; but she had to play her part, and present New Year's gifts to him and the queen, which were by no means a small item in her expenditure. For the present, however, we hear no more of money affairs, and the charming letters which Arabella writes to her uncle and aunt in the north are filled with bits of news and gossip from the court.†

Her spirits appear to have risen with her new position to their natural level, for all evidence tends to show that by nature she was gay and bright, and it seems that her uncle was anxious lest she should be carried away by them. " I trust," she says, " you shall see in me the good

* On December 8, 1604, she received a grant of £1000 per annum, inalienable, for life. Doquet. Calendar of State Papers, Dom., James I., 1603–10, p. 173.

† Part II. C, No. 2, vol. ii. pp. 180–198.

effects of your prayer and your great glory for reforming my untowardly resolutions and mirth . . . which as the best preservative of health I recommend to you." *

In the letter to her aunt of August 23 (p. 169) we find a signal proof of the generosity of her character. She, who had been so coldly and harshly treated by Elizabeth, thanks God that she is no partaker in the mocking talk of those very court ladies who had once flattered the late queen, and now left "no gesture nor fault" of hers "unremembered."

Later on her indignation was doubtless again aroused, when, on the occasion (Christmas, 1603-4) of one of Anne of Denmark's numerous masques, some of Elizabeth's "best apparel" was brought from the Tower to be converted into fancy costumes for the giddy masqueraders.†

In this, the first year of James's reign (1603), the country was devastated by a terrible plague, and the court, pursued everywhere by the infection, was obliged to move about from place to place—a very "camp-volant, which every week

* Part II. C, No. 2, (a), vol. ii. p. 180.   † Ibid., p. 195.

dislodgeth," * as Cecil calls it. But, while the
king's subjects were stricken far and wide by
the terrible "black death," Arabella's letters to
the Shrewsburys tell us of the frivolity—the
hunting, the masques, and games—by which
the new sovereigns and their court passed their
time.

From the correspondence of Sir William
Fowler with the Earl of Shrewsbury at this
time, we hear of Arabella herself. Fowler was
now Anne of Denmark's secretary, and had become intimate with Arabella's relations through
his father, who had been, as we have seen
before (p. 41), executor to her grandmother, the
Countess of Lenox. William Fowler was a
ridiculous personage, at once simpleton and
buffoon ; but, extravagant as is his language,
there is a ring of sincerity about his praises of
the lady, which has led to the supposition that
Fowler would, if he had dared, have joined the
ranks of her suitors. "But I fear I am too
saucy and overbold," he says,† writing from the

* Lodge, "Illustrations of British History," vol. iii. p. 182.
† Ibid., p. 169.

court at Woodstock, September 11, 1603, to
the Earl and Countess of Shrewsbury, "to
trouble your honours; yet I cannot forbear
from giving you advertisement of my great and
good fortune in obtaining the acquaintance of
my Lady Arbella, who may be to the first
seven, justly the eighth wonder of the world.
If I durst I would write more plainly my
opinion of things that fall out here among us,
but I dare not without your lordship's warrant
deal so.   I send two sonnets unto my most
virtuous and honourable lady, the expressers of
my humour and the honour of her whose suffi-
ciency and perfections merit more regard than
this ungrateful and depressing age will afford or
suffer.   The one is a conceit of mine drawn from
an horloge, the other is of that worthy and most
virtuous lady, your niece."   The poem to
Arabella is given here, as a specimen of Fowler's
extravagant admiration of the lady's charms.

> " Whilst organs of vain sense transport the mind,
>   Embracing objects both of sight and ear,
>   Touch, smell, and taste, to which frail flesh inclin'd
>   Prefers such trash to things which are more dear ;
>   Thou godly nymph, possest with heavenly fear,

Divine in soul, devout in life, and grave,
   Rapt from thy sense and sex, thy spirits doth steer
Toys to avoid which reason doth bereave.
O graces rare ! which time from shame shall save,
   Wherein thou breath'st (as in the seas doth fish,
In salt not saltish) exempt from the grave
   Of sad remorse, the lot of worldling's wish.
O ornament both of thy self and sex,
And mirror bright where virtues doth reflex !
      In salo sine sale."

Fowler's cautious words were soon justified by events. Already the clear sky of the new king's reign had been dimmed by gathering clouds. In July a plot, called the Bye or Surprising Treason, got up by two Catholic priests (Watson and Clarke), aided by two Catholic gentlemen (Markham and Copley), had been discovered.

Lord George Brooke and the Puritan Lord Grey of Wilton were deeply implicated ; and Lord Cobham, Brooke's elder brother, with Sir Walter Raleigh, as Cobham's intimate friend, were arrested on suspicion, without, however, any distinct charge being made against them. But in September, Cobham, Brooke, and Raleigh were indicted for another conspiracy, called the Main or Spanish Treason, to distinguish it from the Bye. The object of this Spanish plot was to crush Cecil and the Howards by deposing James, and placing Arabella, whom the conspirators doubtless expected to be a mere tool in their hands, upon the throne. There is no proof * of Raleigh's complicity, in the chief part at least of the design, although he may have been acquainted with vague plots in preparation against the king. James had given him no reason to be satisfied with the change of dynasty, for in consequence of Cecil's enmity, Raleigh had been deprived of his office of captain of the guard, and practically banished from court ever since the new sovereign's accession. As for any connection between the conspirators and Arabella, Sir Walter spoke of her, according to Carleton,† "as of a woman with whom he had no acquaintance, and one whom of all that he saw he never liked," and, indeed, no love was likely to be lost between the rival and enemy of Essex, and one who had boasted of the friendship of that unfortunate

* Gardiner's " History of England," vol. i. p. 79.
† "Court and Times of James I.," vol. i. p. 21.

favourite. The only evidence against Raleigh was furnished by his treacherous friend Cobham, who, although he retracted and apologized for his falsehoods in private, again swore to their truth at the trial. Had it not been for the prejudices of James, and the spite of the overbearing knight's many private enemies, he must have been acquitted of any direct share in either conspiracy.

The trial is wrapped in a good deal of obscurity, since much of the evidence was suppressed; but it is certain that Cobham commissioned his brother to persuade Arabella to write to the Archduke, the King of Spain, and the Duke of Savoy, asking their aid, while promising in return to tolerate the Romish religion in England, and to keep peace with Spain. At the trial, which took place in November at Winchester, Brooke affirmed that " he never did move her as his brother devised," while Cobham said that Arabella had sought his friendship, and his brother Brooke had sought hers,* and that his (Cobham's) only

* " Court and Times of James I.," vol. i. p. 21.

object in seeking for an interview with the lady had been to warn her that there were some about the king that laboured to disgrace her." All the evidence * goes to show that Arabella had taken no part in the plan. Carleton says that "the Lady Arbella, the Archduke, and the King of Spain were merely ignorant of any such thing, which those men had but conceived in their minds and discoursed of among themselves." †

One of Shrewsbury's correspondents writes ‡ him (December 6) an account of Raleigh's trial, in which he says that, though Arabella's name was mentioned in the evidence, " she was cleared in the opinion of all, and, as I heard, my Lord Cecil spake very honourably on her behalf; but one that gave in evidence, as it is said, spake very grossly and rudely concerning her lady-ship." Cecil's words in her defence were, " Here hath been a touch of the Lady Arbella

* See Brooke's Confession, State Papers, James I., Dom. vol. ii. p. 64; and Cobham's Examination, ibid., vol. iii. p. 24, MS.

† "Court and Times of James I.," vol. i. p. 18.

‡ Lodge, " Illustrations of British History," vol. iii. pp. 214-221.

Stuart, the king's near kinswoman.   Let us not
scandal the innocent by confusion of speech.
She is as innocent of all these things as I or
any man here ; only she received a letter from
my Lord Cobham to prepare her, which she
laughed at, and immediately sent it to the king."
"Whereupon the lord admiral,* who was
with the Lady Arbella in a gallery, stood up,
and said, ' The lady doth here protest upon her
salvation, that she never dealt in any of these
things, and so she willed me to tell the court.' " †

The reflections apparently cast upon Arabella's
character at the trial were suppressed, although
the apologetic addresses of the two lords, to
which they gave occasion, were "inadvertently
suffered to be published."   Some suspicions
seem also to have fallen upon Arabella's uncle,
Henry Cavendish, and he was sent for to the
court, witnout, however, being in any way implicated at the trial.

Lord Cobham, who was, as Raleigh called him
at the trial, a "poor, silly, base, dishonour-

---

* The Earl of Nottingham.
† Lodge, "Illustrations of British History," vol. iii. p. 217.

able soul," threw the whole blame of both plots
so successfully upon his brother, that Lord
Brooke lost his head. Cobham himself, Lord
Grey, and Sir Griffin Markham were actually
led out to die at Winchester, while Raleigh,
whose turn was to come a few days later, was
set to watch them from his window; but upon
the very scaffold, when each had gone through
his part, and the axe was about to fall, the
sheriff announced that the king had sent a re-
prieve for all, including Raleigh. This tragi-
comedy was elaborately arranged by James as a
kind of grim practical joke; he took care only to
send a messenger to stop the three executions
at the last moment, and gave special orders that
each victim should be led upon the scaffold, and
only informed of his pardon when all hope
seemed over. But even release from instant
death must have seemed hardly a favour on the
king's part, since the prisoners were remanded
to the Tower, destined to long years of captivity.

Raleigh's fate is well known. Grey, who was
a gallant young lord, with a proud and fiery
spirit, lingered in confinement till 1614, and

then died, broken down and worn out by sickness and captivity, at the age of forty. We shall meet with his name again, but not till after Arabella had joined him in the Tower. Cobham did not die in prison, but his end was base, like his life, his last days being spent in neglect and starvation in a garret, to which the only entrance was by a broken ladder.

When once the trial was over, no further imputations were raised against Arabella's loyalty, and she appears to have risen very high in the king's good graces. The only allusion in her own letters to the subject of the plots is in one written * early in December to her aunt Mary, from Fulston (Foulston, in Kent). The beginning sentence is obscure, but the next is plain enough : " Therefore, when any great matter comes in question," she says, " rest secure, I beseech you, that I am not interested in it as an actor, howsoever the vanity of wicked men's vain designs have made my name pass through a gross and a subtle lawyer's † lips of late, to

* Part II. C, No. 2, (*i*), vol. ii. p. 191.
† Coke, then Attorney-General.

the exercise and increase of my patience, and not their credit."

During the autumn and winter Arabella had been trying to reconcile herself to the frivolities of her new life, so different to the studious and obscure one she had hitherto led. , In this same letter she says, "For if I should not prefer the reading of your kind and most welcome letters before all court delights (admit I delighted as much in them as others do), it were a sign of extreme folly; and liking court sports no better than I do, and than I think you think I do, I know you cannot think me so transformed as to esteem anything less than them." And again, she had also written * a hasty line from Winchester, in October, because she had been sent for to attend some company, and since " I must return at an appointed time to go to my book, I must make the more haste thither."

From the faithful Fowler we hear that she set apart certain hours every day for "lecture, reading, hearing of service and preaching," besides "visiting the princesses." In spite of

* Part II. C, No. 2, (*d*), vol. ii. p. 183.

these occupations, and of constant colds and
weak eyes, she found time to keep the Shrewsburys informed of all that went on, and her
letters to them at this time are full of interest.
The best known of them, written on September
15, from Woodstock, is printed in Lodge's
" Illustrations," * but, though often quoted, it
must not be altogether omitted here, as it is a
good example of her bright and sparkling style.

" I writ to tell you," she says, " of the reason
of the delay of Taxis' audience [the Spanish ambassador, whose audience afterwards took place,
September 24, at Winchester] ; it remaineth to
tell how jovially he behaveth himself in the
interim.   He hath brought great store of
Spanish gloves, hawks' hoods, leather for jerkins,
and, moreover, a perfumer ; these delicacies he
bestoweth amongst our ladies and lords, I will
not say with a hope to effeminate the one sex,
but certainly with a hope to grow gracious with
the other, as he already is.   The curiosity of
our sex drew many ladies and gentlewomen to
gaze at him betwixt his landing-place and

* Vol. iii. pp. 176-178 ; from Talbot MSS., K, 124.

Oxford, his abiding-place; which he, desirous
to satisfy (I will not say nourish that vice), made
his coach stay, and took occasion, with petty
gifts and courtesies, to win soon-won affections,
who, comparing his manner with Monsieur de
Rosney's,* hold him their far welcomer guest.
At Oxford he took some distaste about his
lodging, and would needs lodge at an inn,
because he had not all Christ's College to
himself, and was not received into the town by
the vice-chancellor *in pontificalibus*, which they
never use to do but to the king, or queen, or
Chancellor to the University, as they say; but
those scruples were soon disgested, and he
vouchsafeth to lodge in a piece of the college
till his repair to the king at Winchester.   Count
Aremberg † was here within these few days, and
presented to the queen the archduke and the
infanta's pictures, most excellently drawn.
Yesterday the king and queen dined at a lodge
of Sir Henry Lea's, three miles hence, and were

* De Rosney, afterwards Duc de Sully.

† Count Aremberg, the Austrian ambassador, who was afterwards supposed to have promised his aid to the Main Plot
conspirators.

accompanied by the French ambassador and a Dutch duke. I will not say we were merry at the Dutchkin,* lest you complain of me for telling tales out of the queen's coach; but I could find it in my heart to write unto you some of our yesterday's adventures, but that it groweth late, and by the shortness of your letter I conjecture you would not have this honest gentleman overladen with such superfluous relations.

"My lord admiral † is returned from the prince and princess, and either is or will be my cousin before incredulous you will believe such incongruities in a counsellor, as Love maketh no miracles in his subjects, of what degree or age whatsoever. His daughter of Kildare is discharged of her office,‡ and as near a free woman as may be, and have a bad husband.

* Duke Ulrich of Holstein, afterwards one of her suitors.
† The Earl of Nottingham (see also p. 180). He married Arabella's young kinswoman, Lady Margaret Stuart, at the age of sixty-eight, soon after the date of this letter.
‡ That of state governess to Princess Elizabeth. She was the widow of Lord Kildare, and now the wife of Lord Cobham, whose bad reputation is here alluded to.

"The Dutch lady my Lord Wotton spoke of at Basing proved a lady sent by the Duchess of Holstein to learn the English fashions. She lodgeth at Oxford, and hath been here twice, and thinketh every day long till she be at home, so well she liketh her entertainment, or loveth her own country; in truth, she is civil, and therefore cannot but look for the like which she brings out of a ruder country. But if ever there were such a virtue as courtesy at the court, I marvel what is become of it, for I protest I see little or none of it but in the queen, who, ever since her coming to Newbury, hath spoken to the people as she passeth, and receiveth their prayers with thanks, and thankful countenance, barefaced,* to the great content- ment of native and foreign people ; for I would not have you think the French ambassador would leave that attractive virtue of our late Queen Elizabeth unremembered or uncom- mended, when he saw it imitated by our most gracious queen, lest you should think we infect even our neighbours with incivility.

* The ladies of rank wore black vizards in those days.

"But what a theme have rude I gotten un-
awares! It is your own virtue I commend by
the foil of the contrary vice; and so, thinking
on you, my pen accused myself before I was
aware. Therefore I will put it to silence for
this time, only adding a short but most hearty
prayer for your prosperity in all kinds, and so
humbly take my leave.

"From Woodstock, this 15th September.

"Your lordship's niece,

"ARBELLA STUART."

Directly after his departure she had written *
to assure her uncle that she intends to follow
his directions as far as they are "Puritan-like."
Her resolution must have been difficult to keep
in the midst of a court notorious for its immo-
rality, given up to feasting and revelry, which
too often—as, when later on, the King of
Denmark visited his sister—degenerated into
drunken orgies. Here, where "ladies of high
rank copied the royal manners, and rolled in-

* Part II. C, No. 2, (*a*), vol. ii. p. 180.

toxicated in open court at the king's feet," * no veil of grace and culture was drawn, as in Elizabeth's time, over the vices of the courtiers ; and those who, like Arabella, had been brought up under the old *régime*, must have wished that their former mistress, with all her harshness, might return.

In a diary,† written at this time by a child of about thirteen or fourteen (Anne Clifford, afterwards Countess of Dorset and Pembroke), on her first presentation at the court, we get a contemporary verdict about the new order of things.

After telling how she was taken several times to see " the queen and *Lady Arbella*," while the court lay at Basingstoke, she speaks of a grand masque held at Winchester, and adds that "all the ladies about the court had gotten such ill names, that it had grown a scandalous place, and the queen herself was much fallen from her former greatness and reputation she had in [the] world."

* Green's "Short History of England," p. 473; and see later, pp. 216, 217.
† Seward's "Anecdotes," vol. i. pp. 226, 230.

The following letter* to her uncle, written from Fulston, on December 8, 1603, shows the state of Arabella's feelings on this subject: "I cannot deny so apparent a truth as that wickedness prevaileth with some of our sex, because I daily see some, even of the fairest amongst us, misled and willingly and wittingly ensnared, by the prince of darkness. But yet ours shall still be the purer and more innocent kind. There went ten thousand virgins to heaven in one day. Look but in the almanac, and you shall find that glorious day. And if you think there are some, but not many, of us that may prove saints, I hope you are deceived. But *not many rich, not many noble, shall enter into the kingdom of heaven.* So that riches and nobility are hindrances from heaven, as well as our nature's infirmity. You would think me very full of divinity, or desirous to show that little I have, in both which you should do me wrong, if you knew what business I have at court, and yet preach to you. Pardon me, it is not my function."

The Spanish ambassador, Taxis, must have

* Part II. C, No. 2, (*i*), vol. ii. p. 188.

been a "jovial" man, fond of good company and fair ladies; for Arabella here tells her uncle how he had asked Madame de Beaumont (the French ambassador's lady) to dinner, requesting her to bring some English beauties with her, the famous Penelope, Lady Rich, Essex's sister, being one of those she selected, "and great cheer they had." A fortnight later, the ambassador invited some Scotch nobles, " requesting them to bring the Scottish ladies, for he was desirous to see some natural beauties. My Lady Anne Hay and my cousin Drummond * [Lady Jane] went, and, after the sumptuous dinner, were presented first with a pair of Spanish gloves apiece, and after my cousin Drummond had a diamond ring of the value of two hundred crowns given her, and my Lady Anne a gold chain of Spanish work near that value. My Lady Carey went with them, and had gloves there, and after a gold chain of little links twice about her neck sent her."

The ambassadors were now thronging to

* See later, p. 260.

present their respects to the new sovereign, and envoys from the Turks, the Pope, and the Duke of Savoy were daily expected. The Polonian ambassador would "fain be gone again, because of the freezing of their seas;" and of two envoys sent from Venice, one had already returned to Italy, probably to escape the northern winter.

This same letter winds up with an amusing account * of how the queen and her ladies spent their evenings. "Whilst I was at Winchester, there were certain child-plays remembered by the fair ladies, viz. 'I pray, my lord, give me a course in your park;' 'Rise, pig, and go;' 'One penny follow me,' etc. And when I came to court, they were as highly in request as ever cracking of nuts was. So I was by the mistress of the revels, not only compelled to play at I knew not what (for till that day I never heard of a play called 'Fier'), but even persuaded by the princely example I saw to play the child again. This exercise is most used from ten of the clock at night till two or three in

* Vol. ii. p. 190.

the morning, but that day I made one it began at twilight and ended at supper-time. There was an interlude, but not so ridiculous (as ridiculous as it was) as my letter, which here I conclude."

The rest of the day was spent in masques and other festivities, and besides that the king and queen, being both passionately devoted to hunting, dragged their wretched courtiers after them from place to place in search of the pleasures of the chase, in spite of the open murmurs of the country-folk, whose crops were spoiled and all their provisions eaten up by the royal visitors. At Royston, the king's pet hunting-box, the peasants actually tied a petition to the neck of one of James's favourite hounds, imploring the king—who treated the whole affair as a jest, and took no notice of it—to take himself and his court back to London, for "our provision is spent already, and we are not able to entertain him longer." * The courtiers and court ladies—for ladies were expected to join the chase—also complain bitterly of the "ever-

* Lodge, "Illustrations of British History," vol. iii. p. 245.

lasting hunting," as Arabella calls it in one of her letters * at this time.

The old Earl of Worcester gives a graphic picture † of their very real grievances on the subject. Since he joined the court at Royston, he writes, he has " not had two hours of twenty-four of rest but Sundays; for in the morning we are on horseback by eight, and so continue from the death of one hare to another, until four at night, then, for the most part, we are five miles from home. By that time I find at my lodgings sometimes one, most commonly two packets of letters, all which must be answered before I sleep, for here is none of the Counsel but myself, no, not a clerk of the Counsel nor privy signet; so that an ordinary warrant for post-horses must pass my own hand, my own secretary being sick in London."

* Part II. C, No. 2, (*l*), vol. ii. p. 197.
† Lodge, "Illustrations of British History," vol. iii. p. 247.

CHAPTER IX.

ARABELLA AS A COURT FAVOURITE.

1604–1607.

NEW Year's gifts were a serious item in every courtier's expenditure at that time, even as now, when the survival of the old custom in Christmas-boxes is a tax upon ordinary mortals. Arabella suffered with the rest, and sends very good advice to her uncle and aunt upon the subject. He wished to thank some persons about the court for a service rendered to him, and his niece writes,* "Pardon me if I tell you that I think your thanks will come very unseasonably so near New Year's-tide, especially those with which you send any gratuity. Therefore consider if it were not better to give your New Year's *gift* first to the queen, and your *thanks*

* Part II. C, No. 2, (*i*), vol. ii. p. 188.

after, and keep Mr. Fowler's till after that good time. New Year's-tide will come every year, and be a yearly tribute to them you begin with. You may impute the slowness of your thankfulness to Mr. Hercy,* or me that acquainted you no sooner with your own matter."

To her aunt she writes† the same day, on the same subject, "I asked her [a 'gentle-woman,' whose name is not given] advice for a New Year's gift for the queen, both for myself, who am altogether unprovided, and a great lady, a friend of mine, that is in my case for that matter; and her answer was, the queen regarded not the value, but the device. The gentlewoman neither liked gown nor petti-coat so well as some little bunch of rubies to hang in her ear, or some such daft toy. I mean to give her Majesty two pair of silk stockings lined with plush, and two pair of gloves lined, if London afford me not some daft toy I like better, whereof I cannot bethink me. If I

* The earl's solicitor.
† Part II. C, No. 2, (i), vol. ii. p. 192.

knew the value you would bestow, I think it were no hard matter to get her [the same lady] or Mrs. Hartshide [to] understand the queen's mind without knowing who asked it. The time is spent, and therefore you need lose none of it. I am making the king a purse, and for all the world else I am unprovided. This time will manifest my poverty more than all the rest of the year. But why should I be ashamed of it when it is other's fault, and not in me? My quarter's allowance will not defray this one charge, I believe."

The new year opened with great doings at Hampton Court. Three masques were performed with the customary magnificence, " besides two plays played before the prince," and thirty got up by private persons. The Shrewsburys kept Christmas and New Year at Sheffield, sending their niece a welcome share of their " good cheer ; " but she complains, in a subsequent letter to her uncle, that she is asked "seven times a day at least" when they come to town, and has nothing to say but " *I cannot tell*, which it is their pleasure to believe, and therefore if you will not resolve them nor me of the truth, yet teach me what to answer them." *

That the reconciliation between Cecil and his old enemy still held good we see by the following passage from the next letter : "My Lord Cecil sent me a fair pair of bracelets this morning, in requital of a trifle I presented him at New Year's-tide, which it pleased him to take as I meant it. I find him my very honourable friend both in word and deed. I pray you give him such thanks for me as he many ways deserves, and especially for this extraordinary and unexpected favour, whereby I perceive his lordship reckoneth me in the number of his friends, for whom only such great persons as he reserve such favours" (January 11, 1604). There is a touch of satire in the last sentence, which reminds us of the bitter words which the writer had formerly used about her "honourable friend."

The Shrewsbury family was by no means a pleasant one to belong to, and constant quarrels and money embarrassments forced them all in

* See Part II. D, (*b*) and (*c*), vol. ii. pp. 199, 200.

turn to have recourse to their once ill-treated
relative, whose position at court and growing
influence with the king could now be made use
of for their benefit.   Arabella comes out in a
novel character—that of peacemaker between
her shrewish grandmother and her uncle Gilbert.
She beseeches him in a letter * from Hampton
Court, February 3, 1604, to "put on such a
Christian and honourable mind as best be-
cometh you to bear to a lady so near you and
yours as my grandmother is."   She is in good
hopes, too, of the old lady's "inclination to a
good and reasonable reconciliation betwixt herself and her divided family," and she begs her
uncle, as a personal favour, to allow her to be
"the only mediator and peacemaker" between
him and his step-mother.   "You know," she continues, "I have cause to be partial on your side,
so many kindnesses and favours I have received
from you, and so many unkindnesses and disgraces have I received from the other party."
Referring evidently to her marriage, upon which
subject her relatives had doubtless often tried

* Part II. D, (*d*), vol. ii. pp. 201, 202.

to influence her, she says, " Take as great [power]
over me as you give me over you in this [recon-
ciliation] in all matters but *one,* and in that your
authority and persuasion shall as far exceed
theirs [her other relations] as your kindness
to me did in my trouble," probably in the disgrace of 1603, which would show that if any
coolness had existed between her and the
young Shrewsburys, it was an unimportant
and temporary misunderstanding. Some pro-
jects of marriage were already, as we shall see
further on, in the air, and at the end of the same
letter are referred to in the words, " If you be
weary of me, you may soon be despatched of
me for ever (as I am told) in more honourable
sort than you may deny this my very earnest
request." The request was that the earl would
bring the old Countess of Shrewsbury's eldest
son, Henry Cavendish, and his wife, Grace
Talbot, the earl's own sister, up to town, and
lodge them at his expense, since they could not
afford it themselves, and Arabella herself was
too much out of pocket by her New Year's gifts
to pay their expenses. Why she was so anxious

he should come to town she does not say, but it was for "a good end," and for "my sake and our families' good."

Arabella was now using all her influence at court to help her relations ; both the earl himself and Sir Charles Cavendish were so deeply in debt, and involved in money embarrassments, that they looked to their niece to help, which she most generously did. Sir William Stewart and one Cook, the earl's steward in London, write to tell him and his wife of Arabella's efforts on their behalf. Some lawsuit was evidently impending between the dowager countess and her youngest son, Charles Cavendish, which probably involved Henry too, and accounts for the wish expressed above that he should come to town. Gilbert Talbot, the earl, since his wife was also a Cavendish, had a share in their inheritance, and Arabella threw herself into the breach, as we have seen by her own letter, with all her wonted energy and courage.

The united testimony of Stewart and Cook shows that she was doing her best with the king, though neither of them specify exactly

what her petition was. " In truth," says Stewart,
in a letter * to the earl (February, 1604), " I find
her ladyship both considerate and wise." From
Cook * we have more details (February 12, 1604).
" She hath been even from the beginning very
nobly resolved for Sir Charles Cavendish ; it
is true that, as I marvelled at the fulness of the
reconciliation [with her grandmother] upon
some ground of affection, which notwithstand-
ing is now almost exhaled, so I much feared
what issue the course which her ladyship held
in this would have, for I observed that she
wrestled extraordinarily with my lord duke,
Sir George Hume, and Sir Richard Asheton for
access to the king, and between jest and earnest
rather extorted the same from them by fear than
obtained it by kindness, and having obtained
speech with his Majesty, and I after[wards]
attending her, her ladyship reserved herself . . .
in such sort as that all that she vouchsafed to
intrust unto me was that she was in the king's

* Spencer MSS.   Cook's letter is somewhat imperfect in the
Spencer MSS., but gives names ; while in the Sloane MSS., only
initials are given.

good favour and trusted by him, that she doubted not but you should all find the fruits thereof. . . . But this day her ladyship saith plainly that the king hath been moved and yielded unto her desires, and that she hath entreated his Majesty that in case he shall think it more fit for himself to take the honour of nominating the party than to refer it to her, yet that he will be pleased to take notice of her desire therein, which is absolutely for her uncle Charles, whereunto (she saith) his Majesty hath condescended, and she is to have the same specified under his royal hand on his return from Royston, which it is thought will be about four days hence. Although I must confess," Cook continues, "that this lady permitteth me to treat with her with much less ceremony and awe than I find in myself when I attend some others, yet doth the respect due to such a person prevail with me, so, as in many things which fell from her, good manners led me rather to rest unsatisfied than to interrupt her unreasonably, which is the cause why I cannot ascertain, your honour, whether this motion were made by her-

self to his Majesty when she attended him, or
by some other."

Then follows a reference to the business
which Arabella had undertaken for her uncle,
evidently connected with some money he considered due to him from the old countess.
Cook says he had made "a solemn complaint"
to her ladyship that she had been abused in
the matter of undertaking a reconciliation between her uncle and her grandmother, since at
"the very same instant a motion was secretly
procured for proceeding in the matter of [the]
£4000. . . . My Lady Arbella but this answered:
that my lord should get more than this £4000
of her that sueth." Instead of being any longer
under the old lady's tyranny, Arabella seems to
have most successfully emancipated herself, not
only from her yoke, but from all who had
sought to control her actions hitherto. "Surely,"
Cook continues, "she seems to have mastered
them all that limited her before. She hath
preferred her complaints to his Majesty's ear,
that she can hardly think herself secure in case
she may not have means to speak to his Majesty

without such exceeding endeavours as she had
now been constrained to use, whereupon Sir R.
[Ashton] received, saith she, an extraordinary
check, and her ladyship hath mean[s] hereafter
to speak to the king when it pleaseth her."
Cook concludes this epistle by declaring that
he never saw her ladyship "more cheerful than
this day she was," and by requesting in her
name that the earl would let her have a room
at her disposal at his town house in Broad
Street, "for although she be most resolute not
to lodge from the court, yet may she have many
occasions of such a room."

Whatever was the result of Arabella's petition
to the king, her growing importance at court is
shown by the honourable place assigned to her
in a state procession through the city from the
Tower to Whitehall, on March 15.* As the
king's nearest relative, she rode on a velvet-
caparisoned horse next the queen, taking precedence of all the other noble ladies, and great
must have been the jealousy roused by this
mark of the royal favour.

* Nicholl's "Progresses of King James I.," vol. i. p. 327.

Another proof of her success in her new *rôle*
as a court favourite soon followed. She was in
March appointed carver to the queen, and
writes * from Whitehall shortly afterwards to
her uncle Gilbert about her first attempts to
fulfil the duties of her new office. " I conclude
your lordship hath a quarrel to me," she says,
"and maketh my aunt take it upon her, and
that is (for other can you justly have none)
that you have never a letter of mine since your
going down, to make you merry at your few
spare hours, which, if it be so, your lordship
may command me in plain terms and deserve
it by doing the like, and I shall as willingly
play the fool for your recreation as ever."
Since Lords Cecil, Pembroke, and others write
all the news, "I will only impart trifles to your
lordship at this time as concerning myself.
After I had once carved, the queen never dined
out of her bed-chamber, nor was attended by
any but her chamberers till my Lady of Bedford's return. I doubted my unhandsome
carving had been the cause thereof, but her

* Part II. D, (*e*), vol. ii. pp. 203-205.

Majesty took my endeavour in good part, and
with better words than that beginning deserved,
put me out of my error. At length (for now
I am called to the sermon I must hasten to
an end) it fell out that the importunity of
certain great ladies in that or some other suit
of the like kind had done me this disgrace;
whom should I hear named for one but my
aunt of Shrewsbury, who, they say, at the same
time stood to be the queen's cup-bearer? If I
could have been persuaded to believe, or seem
to believe, that whereof I knew the contrary, I
might have been threatened down to my face
that I was of her counsel therein, that I deeply
dissembled with my friends when I protested the
contrary; for I was heard to confer with her,
they say, to that purpose. But these people do
little know how circumspect my aunt and your
lordship are with me. I humbly thank you for
the example.

"I hear the marriage betwixt my Lord of
Pembroke and my cousin is broken, whereat
sometimes I laugh, otherwhiles I am angry;
sometimes answer soberly as though I thought

it possible, according as it is spoken in simple earnest, scorn, policy, or howsoever at the least as I conceive it to be spoken. And your lordship's secrecy is the cause of this variety (whereby some conjecture that I know something), because I have no certain direction what to say in that case. I was asked within these three days whether your lordship would be here within ten days; unto which (to me) strange question I made so strange an answer as I am sure either your lordship or I are counted great dissemblers. I am none; quit yourself as you may. But I would be very glad you were here, that I need not chide you by letter, as I must needs do, if I be chidden either for the shortness, rareness, or preciseness of my letters, which by your former rules I might think a fault, by your late example a wisdom. I pray you reconcile your deeds and words together, and I shall follow that course herein which your lordship best allows. In the mean time, I have applied myself to your lordship's former liking and the plainness of my own disposition."

There is a tone of annoyance running through

this letter, and it is not the first time that we find Arabella on the brink of a quarrel with her uncle and aunt. They never seem, however, to have gone further than the brink, and Gilbert must have written back a soothing epistle, as he continued on the same friendly terms with his niece. But the allusion to the malice of the court ladies shows us what a difficult part Arabella had to play in the midst of that gossiping, scandal-loving circle.

The Earl of Worcester writes * an amusing description of the quarrels for places amongst the queen's maids of honour to Shrewsbury. " The plotting and malice among them is such," says the frank old soldier, "that I think envy and hatred hath tied an invisible snake about most of their necks, to sting one another to death." But in spite of envious tongues, friends like Sir W. Stewart and Fowler still speak of Arabella in terms of praise. The faithful Fowler, in his usual extravagant language, calls her "more fairer than fair, more beautiful than beauteous, truer than truth itself."

* Lodge, "Illustrations of British History," vol. iii. p. 228.

Moved by her personal attractions, the attraction and charm so largely possessed by the Stuarts, or by purely political motives, many suitors now came forward for Arabella's hand. All of them were, however, rejected, either by the lady herself, or by the commands of her royal cousin, whose fears were always aroused by any idea of her marriage, especially when, as now, the candidates were important foreign princes.

The King of Poland, and Duke Ulrich (the queen's brother), are mentioned as rejected suitors this year (1604), and Fowler, writing * to Earl Gilbert in October, says that the lady herself "will not hear of marriage." He continues his letter with a description of the various attempts made to gain her favour. "Indirectly there were speeches used in the recommendation of Count Maurice, who pretendeth [aspireth] to be Duke of Gueldres; I dare not attempt her." This remark of Fowler's has been construed as a wish to become a suitor himself, but may equally well mean that he dare not plead the cause of the

* Lodge, "Illustrations of British History," vol. iii. p. 236.

count. "The queen's brother, as we hear, has [re]turned to Flushing. The Prince Anhalt has written to me, and albeit he toucheth nothing in his letters that concerns her, yet she nothing liketh his letters nor his Latin. Poland will insist, for his marshal is upon his journey. God give her joy in her choice or destiny!"

The "chief errand" of the King of Poland's ambassador, Shrewsbury's son-in-law, the Earl of Pembroke,* informs him, is "to demand my Lady Arbella in marriage for his master," and so, he adds, "may your princess of the blood grow a great queen, and then we shall be safe from the danger of mis-superscribing letters." It is evident that Arabella's new relation to royalty had caused her correspondents some embarrassment in deciding by what style they should address her—whether as a princess or only as a lady of rank. The King of Poland's ambassador had to return disappointed, for James gave a decided refusal to his master's proposals.

The December of this year (1604) Arabella must have spent in seclusion at Sheffield Lodge,

* Talbot MSS., October 3, 1604.

the Shrewsburys' country seat, since on December 14 her uncle and aunt write * to Cecil that they thank God the measles have dealt so favourably with their niece, and that they have a mistress [a nurse, perhaps] who would not have been so careless of them as the queen that now is."

Some idea of the corruption of the court, and the influence which Arabella still kept over her royal cousin, may be gathered from a curious episode which took place early in the next year (April, 1605), of which the Earl of Shrewsbury was, as usual, informed by letter.† "Mr. Candish [William Cavendish] ‡ is at London, comes to court, and waits hard on my Lady Arbella for his barony; but I am confidently assured that he will not prevail, for I understand that my Lady Arbella is nothing forward in his business, although we be certainly informed that my lady hath a promise of the king for one of her uncles to be a baron;

* Unpublished Cecil Papers, Hatfield.
† Lodge, "Illustrations of British History," vol. iii. pp. 285, 286.
‡ See his letter to the old countess (Hunter's "Hallamshire," p. 122).

but it is not likely to be Mr. William, for he is
very sparing in his gratuity, as I hear,—would
be glad if it were done, but would be sorry to
part with anything for the doing of it . . . I
was with Mr. Candish at my Lady Arbella's
chamber, and he entreated me to speak to my
Lady Bedford to further him, and to solicit my
Lady Arbella in his behalf, but spoke nothing
of *anything that might move her to spend her
breath* for him, so that, by the grace of God,
he is likely to come good speed."

Whether the imputation implied above is a
libel upon the lady, or whether Cavendish
found it possible to be more generous in his
offers, it is certain that, shortly after the date
(April 30, 1605) of this letter, Arabella obtained
the wished-for barony for her uncle, as he is
mentioned among the new-made barons * at the
Princess Mary's christening (May 5, 1605).

Meanwhile the relations between old Bess
and her granddaughter seem to have again
become strained. The part which Arabella had
taken on her uncle Gilbert's behalf in the matter

* Lodge, "Illustrations of British History," vol. iii. p. 280.

of the £4000 had evidently offended the dowager
countess, besides the delay in providing William
Cavendish with his barony.

The hardy virago was gradually succumbing
to the ills of old age—she was now in her
eighty-fifth year ; and, hearing a report * (April,
1605) that she was dangerously ill, Arabella
put aside her private grievances, and hastened
to Hardwick to nurse her. She did not,
however, go quite unprotected from her grandmother's wrath, for she was armed with
a letter from the king himself, asking the
dowager countess to receive her "with her
former bounty and love." Constrained by this
letter, Bess grudgingly bestowed a gold cup and
three hundred pounds upon her needy granddaughter. From the redoubtable old lady's sick-
bed Arabella was summoned to Greenwich for
the christening of Princess Mary (May 5). She
and the Countess of Northumberland were
the godmothers, while the Dukes of Lenox and
Holstein (Arabella's late rejected suitor) were
the godfathers, and a large and brilliant com-

* See Miss Cooper's "Life of Arabella," vol. ii. p. 48.

pany of nobles and noble ladies attended at
the ceremony, Sir William Cavendish, as one of
the newly created barons, helping to carry the
canopy over the baby and her attendants.

Barely two years and a half (she died September 15, 1607) after this glittering scene, the
same little princess was borne quietly to her
grave in Westminster Abbey. She was buried
as cheaply as possible, "without any solemnity
or funeral," by the command of her economical
father. There, in the north aisle of Henry VII.'s
Chapel, we may still see her image, dressed in the
stiff costume of the period, lying upon her tomb,
propped upon one elbow, as in the last moments
of her life, when she raised herself to repeat the
Lord's Prayer, and cry, "I go—I go away—I go."

We read next of Arabella as present with the
king and the court at the Jesuit Garnet's * trial
(April 2, 1606); but the records of her this
year are very scanty, as we have no letters to
the Shrewsburys. Evidently, however, she was
out of pocket, as usual, for in May she writes †

* State Papers, James I., Dom., vol. xx. p. 5, MS.
† Part II. G, No. 1, vol. ii. p. 221.

to Cecil, to ask him to further her suit to the
king for such fees " as may arise out of his seal
which the bishops are by the law to use as I
am informed." She has requested Sir Walter
Cope to recommend this suit of hers to the
minister. She certainly never missed a chance
of adding to her small income, and on March 9,
1607, there is a grant * to her of all sums paid
into the Exchequer from the lands of Thomas,
Earl of Ormond. James had, since his delay
over her pension, acted a generous part by her,
for besides this and other grants, he had even
(in September, 1604) interfered on her behalf
in a lawsuit over the manor of Smallwood, in
Cheshire (see p. 69). The king had written
with his own hand to the Earl of Derby,
Chamberlain of Cheshire, requesting him to
be present at the Assizes, and to take care
that Arabella's cause was not injured. This
year of 1606 the court ladies would be expected to spend a great deal upon their dress,
for in the summer (July), Christian IV., King
of Denmark, the queen's eldest brother, paid a

* Calendar of State Papers, James I., Dom., 1603–10, p. 351.

visit to England, and merry were the revels and also disgraceful the drunken brawls by which his stay at court was celebrated. There were masques or entertainments daily, and so it was no wonder if Arabella found, as seems the case, her debts greatly increased by the end of the year.

James's "poor cousin" made a great personal impression upon the Danish king; and in August, 1606, after his departure, he assures her, through his chamberlain, Sir Andrew Sinclair,* that "there is no honour, advancement, nor pleasure that his Majesty can do your ladyship but he shall do it, faithfully and willingly, as one of the best friends your ladyship has in the world." A present of needlework—"womanish toys," as she calls her work—sent by Arabella to the Danish queen, Sir Andrew tells her, "her Majesty will wear for your ladyship's sake." Arabella writes

* Harl. MSS., 7003, fol. 45, etc. In Part II. E, vol. ii. pp. 209–214, are specimens of this correspondence. Sir Andrew Sinclair addresses one letter (fol. 44) concerning Arabella to his cousin, the Elphinstone she so often alludes to (see her letters to the Shrewsburys in Part II. vol. ii.).

letters full of courtly gratitude for the promise
of the king's protection and favour, to Sir
Andrew, and to the king and queen. She
had also to mediate in a quarrel, which
threatened at first to have serious consequences, since neither party understood the
other's language, between the jovial monarch
and the Lord High Admiral of England,
who took offence at a supposed insult addressed by Christian to his young wife, Lady
Nottingham, just before the king's departure.
The dispute was soon patched up, and, writes *
Sir Andrew to Arabella, "As touching my
Lady Nottingham, the king is now very well
content with her ladyship, because her letter
was written of a little coleric passion founded on
a feckless report."

Early in 1607 the Danish king put Arabella's
"holy friendship" for him to rather a severe
test, since he solicited her, through his sister, to
send him over one of her favourite servants, a
certain Cutting,† who had charmed Christian

* Part II. E, vol. ii. p. 210.
† Probably the famous lute-player of that name (see
" Dictionary of National Biography ").

by his lute-playing. Arabella was away from
court at the time, ostensibly recruiting her
health, at Sheffield ; and Queen Anne wrote *
herself to her on March 9, 1607.   It seems that
Arabella had offended her Majesty in some
way, and was in temporary exile from her
presence, since Anne gives her " the assurance
of our constant favour, with our wishes for the
continuance or convalescence of your health,
expecting your return."   A present was evidently sent by the queen as a token of her
good will ; for in her reply Arabella thanks
her for it, treating it as "an assurance both of
your Majesty's pardon, and of my remaining
in your gracious good opinion."   Meantime
Prince Henry had also written † to Arabella
with the same request ; and she replies to him ‡
and the queen on the same day, March 15, with
a gracious, but regretful, consent.   "Although I
may have seen cause to be sorry," she says, " to
have lost the contentment of a good lute, yet

* Part II. F, (*a*), vol. ii. p. 215.
† Part II. F, (*b*), vol. ii. p. 215.
‡ Letters to the queen and Prince Henry, Part II. F, (*c*)
and (*d*), vol. ii. pp. 216–218.

must I confess that I am right glad to have found any occasion whereby to express to her Majesty and your Highness [Henry] the humble respect which I owe you, and the readiness of my disposition to be conformed to your good pleasures." To the queen also she cannot forbear expressing something of the sacrifice it is to her to let Cutting go; and indeed it was a good deal to ask. "Although I know well how far more easy it is for so great a prince to command the best musicians in the world than for me to recover one not inferior to this, yet do I most willingly embrace this occasion, whereby I may in effect give some demonstration of my unfeigned disposition to apply myself ever unto all your royal pleasures."

To Denmark, therefore, Cutting was despatched (about July), and with him his lady sent some elegant Latin letters, written in her own hand and of her own composition, and addressed to the Danish king, copies * of which

* The draft of an undated one is given in Part II. F, (e), vol. ii. p. 218. Another to the same purport is dated July 15, from Theobalds. There is also a Latin letter to Sir A. Sinclair, Part II. E, vol. ii. p. 214.

are preserved in the Harleian MSS. (7003, f. 37, 52).

A warm friendship had existed for some time between Arabella and her young kinsman, Prince Henry. In 1605 * there is a letter from her to the prince, thanking him for a favour he had done by her "humble suit" to one of her relations; and in 1607 he signs himself her "most loving cousin and assured friend." Birch, the prince's biographer, says that "the Lady Arbella Stuart was not less dear to Prince Henry for her near relation to him than for her accomplishments of mind both natural and acquired; and therefore he took all occasions of obliging her." But, unfortunately, when her troubles come, we shall see that her "assured friend" of 1607 sided with the rest of the world against her.

For the present, however, the family quarrels had ceased; and on July 17 Arabella stood proxy for her grandmother at the christening of the Earl of Arundel's child.† This was the eldest

---

* Part II. D, vol. ii. p. 208.
† Nicholl's "Progresses of King James I.," vol. ii. p. 144.

son of the great art collector and statesman, Thomas Howard, Earl of Arundel, who had married Alethea, third daughter of Gilbert Talbot. The godfather was the king, after whom the boy was called. He died at Ghent, at the age of ten.

Whether through Arabella's means or not, Gilbert was also reconciled to the old lady, and writes * to Cecil, on December 14 (1607), that he, his wife, and Charles Cavendish had just paid a visit to Hardwick Hall, where he found "a lady of great years, great wealth, and great wit which yet still remaineth. She used me with all the kind respect and show of good affection that might be, stayed us there with her one day, and so in all kindness I returned without any repetition or so much as one word of any former suits or unkindnesses ; neither was there any motion on either side, but only compliment, courtesy, and kindness.'

* Unpublished Cecil Papers, Hatfield, vol. cxxiii. fol. 23.

CHAPTER X.

THE FIRST CLOUD.

1608–1610.

EARLY in the new year, Sunday, January 14, 1608, there was a "great golden masque," called the "Masque of Beauty" (by Ben Jonson), performed at court, and Arabella took part in it with the rest of the queen's ladies. Lady Arabella took her place * as usual, till Princess Elizabeth appeared at court, next the queen; after her came her cousin, the Countess of Arundel, and other ladies; these were all received on dry land by the river-god, with great honours.

Chamberlayne, describing the great show of jewels and costumes prepared for this occasion, writes (January 8) † that one lady was said "to be

---

* Nicholl's "Progresses of King James I.," vol. ii. p. 174.
† Ibid., p. 162.

furnished for better than a hundred thousand
pounds . . . And the Lady Arbella goes
beyond her, and the queen must not come
behind." The Spanish ambassador, of whose
liking for beauty we have read, was so pleased
with the way in which the ladies performed
their parts, that he invited fifteen of them,
including Arabella, to dine with him after the
performance, and doubtless sent them home
with presents, as seems to have been his custom.

Both Arabella and her uncle Gilbert had
seen the old Countess of Shrewsbury for the
last time the year before, for on February 13
Bess at last passed away, in her eighty-eighth
year, having survived four husbands. Earl Gilbert
writes to Cecil, on February 14, to tell him
the news, and says that his mother-in-law "had
the blessing of sense and memory to the last;"
he encloses a letter for Arabella (which is no
longer extant) which shows that she was
not present at her grandmother's death-bed.
Many interests were clashing in that chamber
of death, and it was well, perhaps, for Arabella
that she was not in the midst of them. Her

grandmother's last years had been spent "in abundant wealth and splendour, feared by many, beloved by none, flattered by some, and courted by a numerous train of children, grandchildren, and great-grandchildren." *   She had prepared a grand monument for herself in All Hallows' Church, Derby ; but there was some inexplicable delay about the funeral,† since on March 31 Gilbert writes ‡ to Cecil, asking to be let off going to St. George's Feast, as his mother-in-law's funeral is to take place "near St. George's Day." "You will be there so many besides, as I shall not be missed, and I being [able] to do his Majesty no other service by my coming than a short march in a purple robe."

Meantime the Shrewsburys had not remained at Hardwick, for they were on very bad terms with Bess's second son, William, now Lord Cavendish, who took possession of the hall even before the will—which left Hardwick and Chatsworth to him—was read.   They retired to

---

* Hunter's " Hallamshire," p. 100.

† According to the coffin-plate, she was buried on February 16 ("Chronicles of All Saints, Derby," p. 130).

‡ Unpublished Cecil Papers, Hatfield, vol. cxxv. fol. 70.

Sheffield, where Arabella joined them, and on March 1 her uncle writes * to Cecil that she is "somewhat ill at ease." He adds that as yet they are strangers to Lord Cavendish's proceedings, and know nothing of the old lady's will. From the quarrels over Bess's inheritance, which raged among her relations, Arabella kept entirely aloof; she herself had been disinherited by her grandmother after their violent rupture of 1603, and so was able to be neutral. She went from Sheffield to stay at Hardwick, and writes from there, in March, a letter † to her aunt, the Countess of Shrewsbury, with many thanks to her and her uncle Gilbert for "so many kindnesses and favours as I have received at this time of my being *here* [she means while at Sheffield Lodge] from you both, and to take a more mannerly farewell than I could at our parting. . . . In these few lines I will perform that duty (not compliment) of acknowledging myself much bound to you for every particular kindness and bounty of yours at this

* Unpublished Cecil Papers, Hatfield, vol. cxx. fol. 112.
† Part II. G, No. 3, vol. ii. p. 223.

time, which reviveth the memory of many more former [kindnesses]; and to assure you that none of my cousins, your daughters, shall be more ready to do you service than I." The Charles Cavendishes were always favourites of hers, and she sends messages to them and her two pretty cousins, adding, "I think I shall many times wish myself set by my cousin Charles at meals." She and her uncle William had never been on very good terms, but since she had obtained his barony for him, he was obliged to invite her to Hardwick.

By March 23 * she was back in town, and in April we find her name mentioned in connection with the marriage (April 10) of Lord Cavendish's son to a daughter of Lord Kinloss, Master of the Rolls.

Rumour credited Arabella with having been one of the matchmakers, and when her uncle Henry Cavendish taxed her with it, the morning after the ceremony, although she denied the

---

* State Papers, James I., Dom., vol. xxi. p. 86, MS., Shrewsbury to Cecil, enclosing a drawing of Chatsworth Arabella had done for the minister.

charge, it was not "very earnestly;" and Henry adds that he "told her ladyship much my betters would think it as I did, and ten thousand besides." * Pomfret, in his life of the lady,† asserts that the king was the real contriver of the match, but possibly Arabella was his coadjutor. The bride was a "pretty red-headed wench of about thirteen or fourteen, with a portion of £7000;" the bridegroom seems to have been dragged to the altar against his will. The whole affair was so secretly carried out for fear of opposition from high quarters, that nobody but the parties concerned heard of it till after the ceremony, which took place at 8 a.m. in the Chapel of the Rolls. Lord Cavendish then went in person to Whitehall, to invite his niece to the wedding dinner, to which "her ladyship came accordingly," and danced with the rest, "in rejoicing and honour of the wedding." ‡

* Letter from Henry Cavendish to Gilbert Talbot, Sloane MSS., 4161, fol. 19.

† See note in Nicholl's "Progresses of King James I.," vol. ii. pp. 194, 195.

‡ See Lodge's "Illustrations of British History," vol. iii. pp. 351, 352; and Sloane MSS., 4161, fol. 19.

This year Arabella's money difficulties were closing thicker and thicker round her. We find her soliciting the king in the summer for monopolies on oats ; * and in October Chamberlayne reports "the muttering of a bill put into the Exchequer or some other court concerning much land that, by reason of the pretended bastardy of Queen Elizabeth, should descend to divers persons." Arabella is named as one of the chief promoters of the scheme, and Chamberlayne adds, "If there be any such thing, methinks the whole state should rise and resent such an indignity." † The *if* is significant. There is no other evidence against the lady, and the report may have been an entire fabrication ; were it otherwise, it would have been a truly desperate expedient.

The next year (1609)—the last of Arabella's liberty—was not very eventful, though that she

* Lodge, "Illustrations of Bible History," vol. iii. p. 227. On July 25 Bacon has a note : "To remember to be ready for argumentation in my Lady Arbella's cause, before term, and to speak with my Lord of Salisbury about it, chief in point of profit, and the judges to be made and prepared (though my lady be otherwise remembered)" (Spedding's "Life of Bacon," vol. iv. p. 44).

† Nicholl's "Progresses of King James I.," vol. ii. p. 211.

continued in favour is inferred from the fact
that she took part in another famous masque of
Ben Jonson's, the "Masque of Queens," performed at Whitehall on February 2 (Candlemas
Day). We know little more than what can be
learnt from a book * of her expenses, kept by
Hugh Crompton, her steward, and a few letters
which passed between her and the Shrewsburys.
The account-book tells us all the little details
of her living, and gives a very good idea of the
continual calls upon her slender purse †—"the
cost of diet, wages, horse-keeping, masques,
rewards, etc." Besides the household expenses
at Blackfriars, Whitehall, Greenwich Palace, and
other places, the steward gives items of the
money spent in a "visit, or, as in the cases of
persons of the blood royal, it was generally
called, a progress," Arabella made in August
and September (she left Whitehall on August
22, and was at Broad Street on October 10)
among her friends and relations, "principally in

* See a paper by Canon Jackson, in *Wilts. Archæological
Magazine*, vol. xix. p. 217 ; part is given in Part II. G, No. 8.

† Her income this year was made up from sources of her own
to £2160.

Derbyshire." The expenses * chiefly consist of "rewards" paid to the servants of her hosts, and money given to the poor, besides sums spent on hunting, and the shoeing of her horses. Earl Gilbert of Shrewsbury made great preparations at Sheffield for the proper reception of the king's cousin and her train, not treating her merely as his niece, and writes elaborate directions to his steward. "Fish enough must be watered," he says, "for there will be an extreme great number in the hall every day. Fat beefs and fat muttons must be had, and the beef in time killed and powdered. Fat capons provided and reserved till then." †

We have only space to give two more specimens of that sparkling style so characteristic of Arabella's correspondence before misfortune crushed her spirits, which will form a fitting close to the period of unbroken court favour she had now enjoyed for some years.

The first, dated from Blackfriars, November 8,

---

* Which amounted to £323 18*s*., besides some money borrowed on the security of her jewels.

† Hunter's "Hallamshire," p. 124.

1608, is taken from the original manuscript at Longleat. In it we see again the weariness which Arabella had long ago experienced (see her letters in 1603–4) of the frivolous round of her court life, and, by the reference to the lawyers, she seems also to be involved in her usual money difficulties.

"I was much ashamed to be overtaken," she writes to her uncle, "by your lordship's letter by Mr. Fowler, before I had answered your former, but I presume of your pardon for such peccadilloes. Good wishes can never come amiss, whether from amongst cups or beads, and therefore at all adventures I humbly thank your lordship. For want of a nunnery, I have for a while retired myself to the Friars, where I have found by experience this term how much worse they thrive who say, 'Go ye to the plough,' than, 'Go we to the plough,' so that once more I am fettling* myself to follow the lawyers most diligently.

"I pray God the cheese I herewith send your lordship prove as good as great (which few of

* "The word *fettling* means 'preparing.' In Wiltshire, 'to fettle a horse' means to groom him and make him up for the night."—Note by Canon Jackson.

you great lords are, by your leave), and truly
I hope well of it, because the fellow of it which
is tasted here is so.   And as I have sent your
lordship some of the stoppingst meat that is, so
I have sent you some of the sharpest sallet that
ever I eat.   A great person loveth it well (as
I told your lordship at my being with you),
and that is all I can say in commendation of
it.   If you have of it in the country, I pray you
let me know, that I may laugh at myself for
being so busy to get this.   'God send you a
good stomach and a good digestion' shall be
the motto to these two bodies of sallet * and
cheese, I hope with the good allowance of all
the impresa-makers † by North Trent.   And
so beseeching the Almighty to send you all
honour and happiness, I humbly cease.

"Your lordship's niece,

"ARBELLA STUART."

The second letter,‡ which is also addressed

* Salad.

† "An impresa was a stamp, mark, or device, probably used
to distinguish the different kinds of cheese."—Note by Canon
Jackson.

‡ Lodge, "Illustrations of British History," vol. iii. p. 372.

to the Earl of Shrewsbury, is dated from Broad Street, his London house, July 17, 1609.

"Because I know not that your lordship hath forsaken one recreation that you have liked heretofore, I presume to send you a few idle lines to read in your chair, after you have tired yourself either with affairs or any sport that bringeth weariness; and, knowing you well advertised of all occurrents in serious manner, I make it my end only to make you merry, and show my desire to please you even in playing the fool, for no folly is greater, I trow, than to laugh when one smarteth; but that my aunt's divinity can tell you St. Lawrence, deriding his tormentors even upon the gridiron, bade them turn him on the other side, for that he lay on was sufficiently broiled, I should not know how to excuse myself from either insensibleness or contempt of injuries. I find if one rob a house and build a church with the money the wronged party may go pipe in an ivy leaf for any redress; for money so well bestowed must not be taken from that holy work, though the right owner go a-begging. Unto you it is given to under-

stand parables or to command the comment ;
but if you be of this opinion of the Scribes and
Pharisees, I condemn your lordship, by your
leave, for an heretic, by the authority of Pope
Joan ; for there is a text saith, you must not
do evil that good may come thereof.

"But now from doctrine to miracles. I assure
you within these few days I saw a pair of
virginals make good music without help of any
hand, but of one that did nothing but warm,
not move, a glass some five or six feet from
them. And if I thought thus great folk, in-
visibly and far off, work in matters to tune
them as they please, I pray your lordship forgive
me, and I hope God will, to whose holy protection I humbly recommend your lordship. From
Broad Street, June 17, 1609.

"I humbly pray your lordship to bestow
two of the next good personnages of yours
shall fall on me ; not that I mean to convert
them to my own benefit, for though I go
rather for a good clerk than a worldly-wise
woman, I aspire to no degree of Pope Joan,
but some good ends, whereof this bearer will

tell your lordship one. My boldness shows
how honourably I believe of your disposing of
such livings.

> "Your lordship's niece,
>
> "ARBELLA STUART."

Meanwhile, early in 1609, she had sent a
petition to the king for Irish hides to be brought
into the English market, asking licence for herself to export forty thousand hides yearly for
thirty-one years, paying a poundage thereon, and
a rent of £50 per annum. A few months after
she successfully solicits a licence for the privilege
of nominating such persons as shall sell wines
and *aqua vitæ* in Ireland, writing in August *
to thank Lord Salisbury for effecting her suit.
On September 8, 1609, her uncle Gilbert again
expresses her gratitude to the Lord Treasurer,
and adds that she wishes also to have "the
licensing, the brewing, and the sale" of beer
and ale in Ireland.† The grant for the first
request is November 2, 1609, in the Doquet-

---

* Part II. G, No. 5, vol. ii. p. 225.
† State Papers, James I., Dom., vol. xlviii. p. 16, MS

book, and repeated again in the Grant-book, under the date of March 2, 1610; but no mention is made of the second petition. On December 17 Arabella sends another letter * to request Salisbury to use his influence that her patent may speedily pass the Great Seal, which would further the despatch of her suit in Ireland.

Just before Arabella's troubles begin, a significant change takes place in her tone about her money matters—significant if interpreted as a preparation for her approaching marriage. The constant petitions for grants had evidently not sufficed to pay her creditors, for she now writes † to Salisbury (December, no day of the month, but evidently later than the 17th) that she is willing "to return back his Majesty's gracious grant of the monopoly," if her debts may all be paid for her. At the same time, she begs for an increase of her yearly allowance, and asks for an annual thousand pounds instead of her usual diet from the royal table. At the end of the same letter she hints that she has

---

* Part II. G, No. 6, vol. ii. p. 225.
† Ibid., No. 7, vol. ii. p. 276.

other petitions for which she wishes to entreat
the minister's good offices, but that they are
such as " I trust your lordship will think his
Majesty will easily grant."

It must have been only a few days later that
she fell suddenly and mysteriously into disgrace, why we can never exactly know, as the
only allusions to the subject are some passages
vaguely referring to it in contemporary letters.
On December 30 Chamberlayne writes,* " I can
learn no more of the Lady Arbella, but that
she is committed to the Lord Knyvet, and was
yesterday again before the Lords. Her gentleman usher and her waiting-woman are close
prisoners since her first restraint."

That her arrest was connected with money
matters is the simplest explanation, and tallies
with the popular report of the affair. Before
the middle of January she was reinstated in the
king's favour, and on the 20th her usual warrant
for diet was signed.† On February 13 Chamberlayne gives ‡ the following account of her

* Winwood, vol. iii. p. 117.
† State Papers, James I., Dom., 1603–10, Calendar, p. 583.
‡ Winwood, vol. iii. p. 119.

return to favour : "The Lady Arbella's business, whatsoever it is, is ended, and she restored to her former state and grace. The king gave her a cupboard of plate better than £200 for a New Year's gift, and a thousand marks to pay her debts, besides some yearly addition to her income. Want being thought the chiefest cause of her discontentment, though she be not altogether free from the suspicion of being collapsed."

The term " collapsed " is very ambiguous, and the only other light thrown upon the affair is in a letter* from Beaulieu (secretary to Sir Thomas Edmondes) to Trumbull, the British resident at Brussels (February 15, 1610). Here, however, it is so casually referred to, that it probably merely embodied the court gossip, and Beaulieu passes on to a more important subject with which our attention must be henceforth engaged. "The Lady Arbella," he writes, "who (as you know) was *not long ago censured for having, without the king's privity, entertained a motion of marriage,* was again within these

* Winwood, vol. iii. p. 119.

few days apprehended in the like treaty with my Lord of Beauchamp's second son, and both were called and examined yesterday at the court about it. What the matter will prove I know not, but these affectations of marriage in her do give some advantage to the world of impairing the reputation of her constant and virtuous disposition."

Thus we see that, although reinstated in the royal favour, Arabella was destined to lose it again before tongues had ceased to wag about her first disgrace. The year 1609 was the last happy and peaceful time in her life. The royal smile is proverbially a fickle one, and Arabella was henceforth never, except for a very brief space, to bask in its sunshine. The pit was already yawning which was to engulf the unhappy lady, and the rest of her life is but a succession of misfortunes. We must follow her step by step into the fatal consequences her rash love-match was to bring down upon her unlucky head, and see her gradually engulfed and swamped by the ever-rising flood of her misfortunes.

CHAPTER XI.

1610.

THE report of the engagement between Arabella and young Seymour was perfectly well founded, and, indeed, there was little attempt to keep it secret. Seymour, according to his own confession, had not spoken of marriage to the lady till February 2, and scarcely a week had passed before they were both arrested. We know literally nothing about their courtship, but it was probably about Christmas-time, when Arabella had incurred the king's displeasure, that her thoughts were turned to a prospect of marriage with William Seymour. In any case, even if her first disgrace had been because of a marriage project, the hypothesis that it was connected with her debts

being far more likely, no suspicion of an attach-
ment to Seymour can have entered into James's
head.

Early in the new year of 1610, as soon, in
fact, as she was restored to favour, Arabella
obtained a promise from the king that she
might marry whom she pleased, *provided* the
suitor was a subject within the kingdom, and not
a foreigner. The excitement in 1603, when Arabella's name had been coupled with one of Lord
Beauchamp's sons, had long been forgotten, and
James little thought that any fear would again
arise of a union between the Seymours and
Stuarts. To make his promise to let his cousin
marry whom she would the safer, he must have
known that she was not on good terms with the
Earl of Hertford, and evidently William's atten-
tions to his lady had not been conspicuous. In
spite, however, of the fact that no love was lost
between Hertford and herself, no doubt Arabella
had made the acquaintance of the young
Seymours, either when they were at the university or with their father at court.

Both Edward and William Seymour had been

entered on the books of Magdalen College, Oxford, in April, 1605. William took his B.A. on December 9, 1607, and he must have left the university for the court about the next year. There his friendship with the Lady Arabella was cemented and became a warmer feeling, till, with youthful audacity, he dared to make a proposal of marriage to the king's cousin.

What were the motives that dictated this proposal it is hard to say, his whole conduct in the affair being most contradictory. It may have been, as some writers conjecture, from a purely political motive that he sought the hand of the principal lady at James's court. But although Arabella was now thirty-five, she seems to have lost none of her personal attractions, and, since we know for certain that she fell desperately in love with her future husband, the boy of twenty-three would naturally be flattered by the affection of one so much his senior and his superior in rank, and probably for a time at least he returned her sentiments.

On the explosion of the king's wrath, Seymour was, or professed to be, quite ready to relinquish his *fiancée*, and after his arrest * he wrote an apologetic letter † (February 20, 1610) to the Lords of the Council, with an account of the affair, and a humble confession of his error. On Candlemas ‡ Day (February 2) he says he " boldly intruded into her ladyship's chamber in the court," and there the two agreed to plight their troth.

As might have been expected in such a gossiping circle, news of what had taken place soon reached James's ears, and a few days after their engagement both offenders were summoned before the Privy Council. About this time Arabella—since the letter is endorsed " Lady Arbella Stuart," not " Seymour "—must have sent in the undated petition § to the Lords of the Council, in which she begs them to intercede with the king that she might be restored to his favour again.

Whether sincerely or not, Seymour declares in his letter that he would not for worlds attempt

---

* Which took place two days after his *third* meeting with Arabella (see next page).

† Part II. H, No. 1.   ‡ The Feast of the Purification.

§ Part II. H, No. 2.

anything displeasing to the king, and that he
and his lady had originally " resolved not to
proceed to any final conclusion without his
Majesty's most gracious favour and liking first
obtained ; and this [February 2] was our first
meeting.   After that, we had a second meeting
at Mr. Buggs his house, in Fleet Street, and
then a third at Mr. Baynton's, at both which
we had the like conference and resolution as
before."   He further protests, with perfect truth
as we shall see, that " there is neither promise
of *marriage, contract, or any other engagement
whatsoever between her ladyship and myself, nor
ever was any marriage* by me or her intended,
unless his Majesty's gracious favour and appro-
bation might have been first gained therein,
which we resolved to obtain before we would
proceed to any final conclusion."   The words
in italics are underlined in the manuscript, and
several marks scored against them, as if to draw
attention to the important statement therein
contained.

That Seymour was at the time perfectly
sincere and frank in his protestations, and that

he had relied upon the royal promise to Arabella, is shown by a rough draft of a letter, undated and unsigned, addressed to her, which Canon Jackson discovered a few years ago amongst the Longleat Papers. According to this, Seymour was ready and willing to break off the match; and, in the absence of evidence to the contrary, one is reluctantly obliged to believe that Arabella, who was too deeply in love to count the consequences, held him to his plighted word, hopeful that the king would relent when once the decisive step was taken.

William Seymour was indeed a man after the poor lady's own heart, very different to the frivolous courtiers by whom she had been surrounded for so long. He was grave and serious above his years, "loving his book above all other exercise . . . of very good parts, conversant both in the Latin and Greek languages," and remained thoughout his life a man of "studious habits." What wonder that Arabella fell deeply in love with one whose tastes so exactly resembled her own, and events were to prove the correctness of her judgment. In after years her

young lover became one of the most beloved
and respected men at the courts of Charles I.
and at the Restoration, respected, so Clarendon
tells us, even by the opposite party.

Let us turn now to the mysterious letter, by
which we shall see that he strove to free himself
from his dangerous engagement. "I am come,"
says Arabella's unknown correspondent, "with
a message to your ladyship, which was delivered
unto me in the presence of this gentleman your
servant, and therefore your ladyship may be
assured I will neither add nor diminish, but
will truly relate unto you what he hath directed
me to do, which is this. He hath seriously considered of the proceedings between your ladyship and himself, and doth well perceive, if he
should go on therein, it would not only prove
exceedingly prejudicial to your contentment,
but extreme dangerous to him, first in regard
of the inequality of degrees between your ladyship and him, next the king's Majesty's pleasure and commandment to the contrary, which
neither your ladyship nor himself did ever intend
to neglect. He doth, therefore, humbly desire

your ladyship, since the proceeding that is past doth not tie him nor your ladyship to any necessity, but that you may freely commit each other to your best fortunes, that you would be pleased to desist from your intended resolution concerning him, who likewise resolveth not to trouble you any more in this kind, not doubting but your ladyship may have one more fitting for your degree (he having already presumed too high), and himself a meaner match with more security." *

This is certainly not like the language of an ardent lover, but beyond this message, we have only the bare fact of the marriage, and Seymour's own words to Rodney, in which, in direct contradiction to his previous assertions, he declares himself irrevocably bound to marry her ladyship.

That this message was intended, as may be said of the letter to the Council, for the king's edification, is scarcely possible, since it is evidently a private communication. It is only too likely that Arabella's infatuation for the handsome boy overpowered her reason, and that,

* *Wilts. Archæological Magazine*, vol. xv. p. 201.

in spite of all opposition, she insisted on the marriage. That she herself believed both public and private utterances to be merely put on from political motives, is shown by her indignant protest, when Seymour was once accused of fickleness in her presence. He "did no more in this case," she says, "than Abraham and Isaac had done, who disclaimed their wives for a time." *

For the present, however, all seemed over between them. James believed in the sincerity of Seymour's vehement protestations, and both prisoners were released, after promising not to renew their project. Though the engagement was supposed to be over, the gossip about it had not ceased, and James was probably the only person about the English court who imagined all danger of its renewal to be past.

Lord Dunfermline writes,† on March 31, to Salisbury, to thank him for his tidings of the Lady Arabella. "We have much talk of her business here [in Edinburgh], but, indeed,

---

* "Court and Times of James I.," vol. i. p. 126.
† State Papers, James I., Dom., vol. liii. p. 55, MS.

amongst divers rumours of that matter . . .
the most constant report we had here was of
her intention to have married a younger son of
Lord Beauchamp. This was written by sundry
there, and by some (who) might have seemed to
have responsible knowledge and intelligence of
Arbella's affairs—a great argument not to give
trust to reports in matters of importance, for
on light conjecture and weak ground strong
assertions will be builded and go far ahead."

Meantime Arabella had been restored to all
her privileges as before, and nearly three months
passed before Seymour finally resolved to keep
troth to his lady rather than to his sovereign.

About Whitsuntide, meeting a friend of his
at Lambeth, he told him that "he found
himself bound in conscience, by reason of a
former pledging of his faith to her [Arabella],"
and that he had resolved to marry her. He
did not, however, tell his friend "the means
which he used in the reobtaining of her love,
nor once mentioned unto me either letter,
token, message, or aught else which had passed
between them, . . . seeming to me to fear no

other let nor obstacle than his grandfather, my Lord of Hertford." *   At the same time, he bound his confidant by a solemn oath to reveal nothing of all this till he absolved him.   The friend was a certain Edward Rodney, a young man whom the Earl of Hertford looked upon with great dislike, as an evil companion for his grandson.

From that time till June 21 Rodney heard no more of his friend's plans, but on that day Seymour came to fetch him to witness his marriage, and Rodney consented, " nothing doubting," so he says in his examination, "of the king his consent."

The two friends then went by boat to Greenwich, where Arabella was at that time residing, and, reaching there at midnight, they sat up in the lady's chamber till between three and four in the morning, when the marriage was solemnized (Friday, June 22, 1610).   Four of Arabella's servants—Kyrton, Reeves, Mrs. Biron, and Mrs. Bradshaw †—were witnesses of the

* Abstract of Rodney's Confession, written by himself. Harl. MSS., 7003, fol. 62.
 † *Wilts. Archæological Magazine,* vol. xv. p. 201.

ceremony, besides her gentleman usher and steward, Hugh Crompton, who has left in a fly-leaf of an account-book the only record, except Seymour's own confession, of the exact date upon which the marriage took place. Canon Jackson found this account-book,* amongst other papers relating to Arabella and Seymour, at Longleat. "One Blague, son to the Dean of Rochester, was the minister that married them." †

Meanwhile, in spite of the agitation that the arrangements for this secret marriage must have involved, especially if Seymour were unwilling to take such a serious step, Arabella went through the routine of her court life as if nothing unusual were taking place. The last time we hear of her appearance at a court ceremonial was on June 4, 1610, at the creation of her friend and cousin Henry as Prince of Wales. The queen gave a grand masque called "Tethys' Festival," ‡ or "The Queen's Masque," written by Samuel Daniel, the dresses designed

---

* *Wilts. Archæological Magazine,* vol. xv. p. 201.
† Seymour's Confession, vol. ii. p. 281.
‡ Nicholl's "Progresses of King James I.," vol. ii. p. 348.

by Inigo Jones, in honour of the occasion ; and once again Lady Arabella took a leading part, coming next in the procession to Princess Elizabeth. ´

The queen personated Tethys, queen of the ocean, the other ladies being the rivers. Arabella was nymph of the Trent, and wore one of those extravagant costumes which added so much to her money difficulties. The "head-tire" of the river-nymphs, we read, was "composed of shells and coral," the long skirt, "wrought with lace, waved round about like a river, and on the banks sedge and sea-weeds, all of gold."

But the final catastrophe was fast approaching. Early in July all was discovered, and the newly married pair were arrested on July 8, and thrown into prison. Carleton writes to Winwood that "the great match which was lately stolen betwix the Lady Arbella and young Beauchamp provides them both of safe lodgings : the lady close prisoner at Sir Thomas Parry's * house at Lambeth, and her husband in the Tower." †

---

* Parry was Chancellor of the Duchy of Lancaster. See warrant to Parry in Part II. H, No. 3, vol. ii. p. 241.

† Winwood, vol. iii. p. 201.

A Nonconformist minister,* one Melville, who had been imprisoned for four years, on account of some jeering words he had used about the altar † in the Chapel Royal, greeted Seymour upon his arrival in the Tower with a Latin distich, the "pretty quaintness" of which may compensate for the momentary interruption of the narrative, especially as we find in it the modern spelling of Arabella's name.

"Communis tecum mihi causa est carceris ; Ara-
-Bella tibi causa est, araque sacra mihi."
("From the same cause my woe proceeds and thine ;
Thy altar lovely is, and sacred mine.")

Reeves and Crompton were imprisoned in the Marshalsea, for the fault of having been witnesses of the wedding, and, by a letter ‡ of Earl Gilbert's, the steward seems to have been in a precarious state of health. "If Crompton should perish," he says, "the poor lady would be infinitely distressed, he being the man in whom she most reposed her trust touching her debts."

* Winwood, vol. iii. p. 201.
† "Romance of the Peerage," vol. ii. p. 376 ; and Gardiner's "History of England," vol. i. p. 319.
‡ See note next page.

From the faithful devotion he displayed later on, and also the careful accounts he has left us of Arabella's money affairs, we can easily under- stand what a valuable servant he must have been to his mistress. In the midst of her own anxieties, Arabella did not forget those who were suffering for her sake, and she wrote to the Lords of the Council—the letter is dated August 10, from Milbrook, showing she was not as yet a very close prisoner—to beg that these two servants might be removed from the Marshalsea to a more "healthful air," since she hears that "divers near that prison and in it are lately dead, and divers others sick of contagious and deadly diseases." * Her uncle Gilbert also petitioned Lord Salisbury on their behalf.†

The poor lady employed the long hours of her captivity in writing petitions and letters ‡ on her own behalf to the king, the queen, and her relatives and friends at the court. We gather the embarrassed state of her money affairs, as well as her fear that, whatever the result, her

* Part II. H, No. 6, vol. ii, pp. 243, 244.
† State Papers, James I., Dom., vol. lvii. p. 13, MS.
‡ Part II. H.

case would drag on a long while, by a letter * to
her uncle Gilbert (from Lambeth, July 16), in
which she begs him to dismiss her household,
because, by reason of the greatness of her debts,
she can no longer maintain herself and them.
She also asks her uncle to accept her "bay
gelding"—probably "Bay Briton," or "Bay Fen-
ton," one of the horses she had with her on her
progress in 1609—and the rest of her stable. A
few days after (July 19),† she writes again to the
earl, to thank him for his care in disposing of
her servants, and begging him to intercede for
her with the king. Her petitions to the king
himself would have touched the heart of any
one but the cold and unfeeling James, who
seems not even to have vouchsafed a reply.

There are several copies of different petitions
to the king amongst the Harleian MSS., written
in her own clear hand or in the crabbed charac-
ters of her secretary, but unfortunately there are
no dates affixed, and, as with the numerous
letters and fragments of letters to friends at

* Part II. H, No. 5, vol. ii. p. 243.
† Ibid., No. 4, vol. ii. p. 242.

court she wrote during her imprisonment either
at this period or later from the Tower, it is
extremely difficult, indeed almost impossible, to
place them in their right order. Wherever no
date is affixed, the internal evidence is followed,
and for this reason the most despairing letters
are placed after her abortive escape, and removal
to the Tower.

In one petition to the king, probably written
soon after her arrest, while lamenting her hard
fortune in having offended his Majesty, she adds
with much spirit a defence of her so-called
crime. "And though your Majesty's neglect of
me, my good liking * of this gentleman that is
my husband, and my fortune drew me to a contract before I acquainted your Majesty, I humbly
beseech your Majesty to consider how impossible it was for me to imagine it could be offensive unto your Majesty, having few days before
given me your royal consent to bestow myself
on any subject of your Majesty's (which likewise your Majesty had done long since). Besides, never having been either prohibited any,

---

* "Love" in rough draft.

or spoken to for any in this land by your Majesty these seven years that I have lived in your Majesty's house, I could not conceive that your Majesty regarded my marriage at all ; whereas if your Majesty had vouchsafed to tell me your mind and accept the free-will offering of my obedience, I could not have offended your Majesty, of whose gracious goodness I presume so much that, if it were as convenient in a worldly respect as malice may make it seem, to separate us whom God hath joined, your Majesty would not do evil that good might come thereof, nor make me, that have the honour to be so near your Majesty in blood, the first precedent that ever was, though our princes may have left some as little imitable for so good and gracious a king as your Majesty, as David's dealing with Uriah." *

There are two other petitions † to the king, probably written from Lambeth, but later than this one, since they are much more humble in tone, and, as the winter drew on, the poor lady may

* Harl. MSS., 7003, fol. 82, rough draft ; fol. 57, copy.
† Part II. H, Nos. 10 and 11, vol. ii. pp. 248, 249.

well have grown less hopeful of pardon. Yet
in one * she again dwells upon the fact that,
since the marriage had taken place, she and
Seymour were one before God, and implies
that, in justice, they could not now be separated. " My own conscience witnessing before
God," she says, "that I was then "—referring to
the period after her engagement and before the
marriage ceremony, an important fact, if it means
that they had been plighted without reservation
to each other before the king's prohibition—
" the wife of him that now I am.   I could never
have matched with any other man, but to have
lived all the days of my life as an harlot, which
your Majesty would have abhorred in any,
especially in one who hath the honour (how
otherwise unfortunate soever) to have any drop
of your Majesty's blood in them."

That Anne of Denmark, in spite of her easy,
flighty nature, was really touched by Arabella's
distress, and did her best to help her, without, however, making any impression upon her
husband's obstinacy, we see by two grateful

* See Part II. H, No. 10, vol. ii. p. 248.

letters Arabella wrote the queen, and the fact that she sent all her petitions to the king through his wife.

On July 23, 1610,[*] she writes, " Since I am debarred the happiness of attending your Majesty, or so much as to kiss your royal hands, pardon my presumption in presenting your Majesty in this rude form my most humble thanks for your Majesty's gracious favour and mediations to his Majesty for me, which your Majesty's goodness (my greatest comfort and hope in this affliction) I most humbly beseech your Majesty to continue."   In October she again addresses the queen,[†] begging for her continual favour and mediation on her behalf, and enclosing one of her petitions to the king, both documents being enclosed in a letter [‡] to one of the court ladies, Lady Jane Drummond.

Lady Drummond's letters are unfortunately undated, but it is evidently after receiving the above that she writes [§] to Arabella : " . . . this day

---

[*] Lansd. MSS., 1236, fol. 58.
[†] Part II. H, No. 9, vol. ii. p. 246.
[‡] Ibid., No. 12, vol. ii. p. 250.
[§] Ibid., No. 13, vol. ii. p. 251.

her Majesty hath seen your ladyship's letter. Her Majesty says that when she gave your lady-ship's petition to his Majesty, he did take it well enough, but gave no other answer than that ' *Ye had eaten of the forbidden tree.*' This was all her Majesty commanded me to say to your ladyship in this purpose, but withal did remem-ber her kindly to your ladyship, and sent you this little token in witness of the continuance of her Majesty's favour to your ladyship. Now, where your ladyship desires me to deal openly and freely with you, I protest I can say nothing on knowledge, for I never spoke to any of that purpose but to the queen ; but the wisdom of this state, with the example how some of your quality in the like case has been used, makes me fear that ye shall not find so easy end to your troubles as ye expect or I wish."

Arabella writes * back a grateful letter to Lady Jane in return for the royal favour, pray-ing her to "present her † Majesty this piece of

---

* Part II. H, No. 14, vol. ii. p. 252.

† In Lewis's "Clarendon Gallery," vol. ii. p. 333, this letter is put later, *her* being taken for *his*.

my work, which I humbly beseech her Majesty
to accept in remembrance of the poor prisoner,
her Majesty's most humble servant, that wrought
them, in hope those royal hands will vouchsafe
to wear them, which till I have the honour to
kiss, I shall live in a great deal of sorrow. I
must also render you my kindest thanks for
your so friendly and freely imparting your
opinion of my suit. But whereas my good
friends may doubt my said suit will be more
long and difficult to obtain than they wish by
reason of the wisdom of this state in dealing
with others of my quality in the like cause, I
say that I never heard nor read of anybody's
case that might be truly and justly compared to
this of mine, which, being truly considered, will
be found so far differing as there can be no true
resemblance made thereof to any others ; and
so I am assured that both their Majesties (when
it shall please them duly to examine it in their
princely wisdoms) will easily discern. And I
do earnestly entreat you to move her Majesty
to vouchsafe the continuance of her so gracious
a beginning on my behalf, and to persuade his

Majesty to weigh my cause aright, and then I shall not doubt but speedily to receive that royal justice and favour that my own soul witnesseth I have ever deserved at his Majesty's hands, and will ever endeavour to deserve of him and his whilst I have breath."

Besides these petitions and letters to the king and queen, Arabella had addressed the Lords of the Privy Council, before and after the examination of "all the parties" connected with her "error," as she calls the crime she had committed in venturing to oppose the royal mandate. Both these petitions, as her other letters during her imprisonment, seem to us nowadays written in extravagantly servile terms as regards the king's displeasure.

In the first * (July, 1610) she declares she would "endure with alacrity" any "imprisonment or other affliction," "if it were to do his Majesty service or honour, . . . on whose favour all my worldly joy as well as my fortune dependeth." In the second,† written

---

* Part II. H, No. 7, vol. ii. pp. 244, 245.
† Ibid., No. 8, vol. ii. pp. 245, 256.

after the examination, and after she had tasted "restraint from liberty, comfort, and counsel of friends, and all the effects of imprisonment," she again affirms she would endure all "with patience and alacrity," if it were not that, "inflicted as a sign of his Majesty's displeasure, it is very grievous for us."

Before condemning the insincerity of this excess of humility, we must remember that not only was it the custom of the day to speak thus extravagantly of the loss of the royal favour, but that this was the only way by which the captive could hope to mitigate the king's wrath. It would have been of no avail had she painted her misery as proceeding from her separation from her bridegroom; her best policy, as she who had lived all her life in the atmosphere of courts well knew, was to represent the withdrawal of the royal smile as the chief and indeed only cause of her present despondency. But as Lady Drummond truly hints, she might have learnt, from the example of the sad fate and separation of her husband's grandfather and grandmother (Hertford and

Katharine Grey), that when policy and fear
had the upper hand of mercy and justice in
a sovereign's mind, there was little hope of a
mitigation of their decree. Had Arabella
known what was in store for her, she would
have prayed, not that her forlorn condition
might be kept, by the supplications of herself
and her friends, before the king's mind, but
that he might forget her and leave her in
peace at Lambeth. There, at any rate, by the
kindness of her lenient keeper, Sir Thomas
Parry, she was treated more as a guest than
a prisoner. She was allowed to walk about
the garden, and was attended by a certain
number of her old servants, and through one
of them, a certain "Smyth," was able to carry
on a secret correspondence with her husband.

Seymour, on the plea of decaying health
from his "long and close imprisonment,"
addressed a petition,* praying for the liberty
of the Tower, to the Lords of the Council;
and that his request was granted seems most
probable, since later on he was able to elude

* Harl. MSS., 7003, fol. 113.

his keepers with ease, showing that he was allowed a certain amount of freedom. Indeed, it is not impossible that, while his wife was at Lambeth, he may have slipped down the river in a boat, and had stolen interviews with her; but this is mere conjecture. That they corresponded is certain, but unfortunately, the only remaining sample of this correspondence is a letter of Arabella's to her husband; *none* of his to her are extant. It would have been interesting to see if the private expressions of his devotion, especially now the die was cast and no recantation was possible, were more satisfactory than his public protestations.

That as yet, with the exception of his crusty old grandfather, Seymour's family had stood by both him and his wife, is shown by two grateful letters * from them both to his brother Francis, written evidently about the same time; Seymour's bears the date of November 4, 1610. Both praise Francis for his friendship to them,

* Unpublished MSS. sold at Sotheby's, March 16 and 17, 1888.

but if the "my lady" in the following passage
from Seymour's epistle were to be interpreted as
his wife, there would be a sad difference in tone
to hers about him.   It is much more probable,
however, that he refers to her aunt Mary of
Shrewsbury, who, while remaining on Arabella's
side, no doubt injured her cause by her violence
on her behalf; for Mary had inherited all her
mother Bess of Hardwick's scheming, ambitious character.   After speaking of his grandfather, Seymour says, "As for my Lady
[Shrewsbury] I can expect no good from her,
since I am credibly informed that she doth
more harm than good, as I can in some
particulars evidently prove; but I am not
deceived in her, since I never expected other
from her." The tone of the letter makes it
certain that, whoever Seymour refers to, it
cannot be his wife.

Arabella's letter is addressed to her honourable good brother, Mr. Francis Seymour.   In
it she says she hopes that "howsoever higher
powers cross the greatest part of my happiness in depriving me for a time of your dear

brother, my husband, I may not be altogether
a stranger to your family, and yourself in particular, whose extraordinary kindness in this
time shall be requited, God willing, with the
redoubled love of so near alliance and obliga-
tion. I will endeavour to make my patience
deserve excuse, if not consideration, at your
hands ; but it is the virtue I wish may be
best put to proof in my friends, of all others."
She speaks also of her husband's constancy.

We must now give Arabella's only extant
letter * to William himself, as a further proof
of her love for him, and of the courage with
which she bore her trials, and dared to hope
against hope.

"SIR,

"I am exceeding sorry to hear you have
not been well. I pray you let me know truly
how you do, and what was the cause of it ; for
I am not satisfied with the reason Smith gives
for it. But if it be a cold, I will impute it
to some sympathy betwixt us, having myself

* Harl. MSS., 7003, fol. 150.

gotten a swollen cheek at the same time with a cold. For God's sake let not your grief of mind work upon your body. You may see by me what inconveniences it may bring one to. And no fortune, I assure you, daunts me so much as that weakness of body I find in myself; for 'si nous vivons l'âge d'un veau,' as Marot * says, we may, by God's grace, be happier than we look for in being suffered to enjoy ourselves with his Majesty's favour. But if we be not able to live to it, I, for my part, shall think myself a pattern of misfortune in enjoying so great a blessing as you so little a while. No separation but that deprives me of the comfort of you, for, wheresoever you be, or in what state soever you are, it sufficeth me you are mine. Rachel wept, and would not be comforted, because her children were no more ; and that, indeed, is the remediless sorrow, and none else. And therefore God bless us from that, and I will hope well of the rest, though I see no

* Clement Marot, the fashionable poet at the courts of François I. and his sister Marguerite d'Angoulême, Queen of Navarre. It probably refers to the epitaph on Jan le Veau, as pointed out by Lady Theresa Lewis, "Clarendon Gallery," vol. ii. p. 302.

apparent hope. But I am sure God's book mentioneth many of His children in as great distress that have done well after, even in this world. I assure you, nothing the State can do with me can trouble me so much as the news of your being ill doth. And you see when I am troubled, I trouble you too with tedious kindness, for so I think you will account so long a letter, yourself not having written to me for this good while so much as how you do. But, sweet sir, I speak not this to trouble you with writing but when you please. Be well, and I shall account myself happy in being your faithful, loving wife,

"ARB. S."

Unfortunately, the indulgence of the prisoner's gaoler came round to the king's ears after Arabella had been seven or eight months at Lambeth. Incensed by the lax manner in which his commands regarding the strict seclusion * of the prisoner had been obeyed, James ordéred

* See the warrant (Part II. H, No. 3, vol. ii. p. 241) delivering Arabella over to Parry's charge, in which it is expressly said that no person should have access to her until his Majesty's pleasure be known.

Sir Thomas Parry to resign his charge, giving *
him £300 to pay the expenses he had incurred
by entertaining her and her five servants.

On March 13 (1611) the King wrote with his
own hand a letter† to Dr. William James,
Bishop of Durham, committing the person of
his cousin, the Lady Arabella, to that prelate's
"care and custody." The letter expresses the
royal indignation with the rebellious lady, who
had dared to wed, not only without the king's
knowledge, but also with a person whom "he
had expressly forbidden her to marry, after he
had, in our presence and before our Council,
foresworn all interest as concerning her, either
past or present, with protestations upon his
allegiance, in her own hearing, never to renew
such motion again."

Truly James, outwitted in such a barefaced
manner, had good reason for his wrath; but it
was a pity, since the irrevocable step had been
taken, he persistently ignored the impossibility
of undoing the mischief, and continued his harsh

* Part II. H, No. 17, vol. ii. p. 255.
† Ibid., No. 18, vol. ii. p. 257.

measures, forgetting that love laughs at bolts and bars.

This same letter winds up with many hypocritical assurances of the king's wish to temper the severity of his justice with grace and favour, as proved by his sending his unruly cousin to the bishop's house, where " she may be so well assured to receive all good usage, and see more fruit and exercise of religion and virtue than in many other places." But the motive for this change of residence is easy to discover, and Arabella well understood that her removal to the north was intended to place a hopeless barrier between herself and her husband, by carrying her so far away from him.

One more effort she made to obtain a fair trial by an appeal to the Lord Chief Justice of England and the Lord Chief Justice of the Common Pleas. The tone of the petition * is noble in its simplicity, and by the reliance she still puts in the hope of justice being done to her. Before she is removed far from the courts of justice to remote parts, she begs the judges

* Part II. H, No. 16, vol. ii. p. 254.

"to inquire by an Habeas Corpus or other usual form of law what is my fault ; and if, upon examination by your Lordships, I shall thereof be justly convicted, let me endure such punishment by your Lordships' sentence as is due to such an offender.   And if your Lordships may not or will not of yourselves grant unto me the ordinary relief of a distressed subject, then I beseech you become humble intercessors to his Majesty that I may receive such benefit of justice as both his Majesty by his oath, those of his blood not excepted, hath promised, and the laws of this realm afford to all others.   And though, unfortunate woman (that I am), I should obtain neither, yet I beseech your Lordships retain me in your good opinion, and judge charitably till I be proved to have committed any offence, either against God or his Majesty, deserving so long restraint or separation from my lawful husband."

But at that time it was not easy to obtain justice against the king's will, and this appeal to the law of the land was entirely disregarded.

One of Arabella's friends and pensioners, a Mrs. Alice Collingwood, applied to her for help * in March, before she left Lambeth, evidently knowing nothing of the immediate distress her patroness was in, but appealing to her sympathy on the ground of a common trouble—her detention from her lawful husband. This was probably the Francis Collingwood,† a recusant, who was examined on a charge of slandering the king in December, 1606, and was no doubt still in prison. The whole letter shows how confidently the poor lady expected substantial help and also sympathy from Lady Arabella, although she was so much below her in rank. The captive certainly cannot have been able to help another, as she was in a worse predicament herself, and her mind filled with the projected journey to the north.

* See letter in Part II. H, No. 20, vol. ii. p. 259.
† State Papers, James I., Dom., 1606, vol. xvi. p. 51 ; vol. xxvi. p. 20.

END OF VOL. I.

PRINTED BY WILLIAM CLOWES AND SONS, LIMITED, LONDON AND BECCLES.   *D. & Co.*

www.ingramcontent.com/pod-product-compliance
Lightning Source LLC
Chambersburg PA
CBHW020858020726
47497CB00005B/1461